BREAKING
THE RULES

What Reviewers Say About
Larkin Rose's Work

Kiss the Rain

"In this story Larkin Rose has created two awesome leading women who in their own way tower over everyone. I was truly dazed at the beginning and continued to be astounded throughout the novel. …I can, without a doubt, recommend this book for the extraordinary strength and stunning depth that each noteworthy woman presented to me over and over again. Transcendent! [The conclusion] sent me soaring and believing in miracles. This book is like ambrosia and a nearly perfect kiss among Eve, Jodi, and the rain. Incredibly satisfying!"—*Rainbow Book Reviews*

"Even if you're not a fan of erotica, Larkin Rose is an expert at knowing how to keep you turning the pages. *Kiss the Rain* is the story of what happens when Jodi and Eve meet during London's Fashion Week. It also tells how lives can change in seven days. The sex is extremely hot, and the tension is high. This is an enjoyable read which is perfect for a beautiful spring day."—*Just About Write*

I Dare You

"Oh my goodness. Well, this is quite a lovely leap and a jump from Ms. Rose's first book. Gritty, sexy as all get-out, and broadcasting her leading women's passions, doubts, and strengths all over the place. I wouldn't want it any other way. Kelsey and Jordan are very strong characters and it is hard to imagine them not burning each other out or obliterating each other from the face of the earth. I found this pairing incredibly refreshing and provocative."—*Rainbow Book Reviews*

"Rose's well-crafted debut novel is erotica with benefits—plausible plotting, a fast pace, and well-defined secondary characters, including an engaging gay drag queen whose sturdy shoulder is always there when Kelsey needs grounded queer advice."—*Q Syndicate*

No Leavin' Love

"This story feels like an allegory and from that viewpoint it soars, dips, spins wildly around its central theme, and certainly touched my own heart's periodic desire and longing to go home. These are two powerfully impressive women, who pretty much met their match between them. I certainly recommend you stay the course, enjoy the wedding, and then discover when or how the loose ends get resolved. Marvelously pleasurable!"—*Rainbow Book Reviews*

Visions

"Past intertwines with present in Rose's (*Kiss the Rain*) charming new erotic romance. Fortunately, the seduction unfolds with enough spice and sweetness to keep readers satisfied."—*Publishers Weekly*

"I howled, applauded, panted, and dabbed away the tears from pure pleasure while reading this book. This is a wonderful multi-layered love story, peppered with nearly devastating confusion, and practically undermined by misunderstood class collision. I think it would be divine to see this as a play or movie, but the remarkably pure sexual heat would definitely limit the distribution venue. What a shame. At least there is the written word and that has masterfully unraveled the intimacy and details allowing me to savor the humor, the women, and the monumental obstacles seeking to crumble the wishes and desires for the star-crossed characters. I unquestionably recommend this!"—*Rainbow Book Reviews*

Vapor

"This story possibly takes the ultimate award in having two people completely misconstrue each other. Plus, they never talk about it. Of course, with the super sizzling action between the sheets, on the staircase, in the washroom, who really has time to discuss anything? Brilliant, engaging, funny, tearful, and loaded with love, I was beguiled from the very beginning. Hats off to Larkin Rose, another Bold Strokes Books author, for masterminding this marvelous book."—*Rainbow Book Reviews*

By the Author

I Dare You

No Leavin' Love

The Pleasure Planner

Vapor

Kiss the Rain

Visions

Breaking the Rules

BREAKING THE RULES

by

Larkin Rose

2018

BREAKING THE RULES
© 2018 By Larkin Rose. All Rights Reserved.

ISBN 13: 978-1-63555-261-4

This Trade Paperback Original Is Published By
Bold Strokes Books, Inc.
P.O. Box 249
Valley Falls, NY 12185

First Edition: October 2018

CREDITS
EDITOR: CINDY CRESAP
PRODUCTION DESIGN: SUSAN RAMUNDO
COVER DESIGN BY TAMMY SEIDICK

Dedication

To Kevin, for sharing Delaney's with us, and for having the coolest Irish Pub Spartanburg has ever seen.

To my dad, who swears he doesn't read my books, then gets caught stealing them. Biggest compliment ever! I love you for that.

To Toni, my faithful "you're head-hopping, stop that!" book reading partner. I adore you!

To Rad, the coolest boss ever, who believes that the crap in my head is worthy of ink. Thank you!

And finally, to Rose, the rotation to my world, who is eagerly waiting to retire with #10, I love you more and you know it!

CHAPTER ONE

Virginia "Gin" Ward growled at the computer screen while an impact wrench whined in the background. Normally, that sound helped her focus on edits, helped her turn a bad ending into comic relief. Today, not so much.

Forming sentences for the new article about her latest date was driving her insane. She wasn't a writer, dammit. She just wanted to get to the point about how her date night had been an endless waste of time, how she knew immediately that the woman was a waste of space, how the air she breathed would be better spent on a slug, and how to provide her readers with the insight to spot the identical traits in their own encounters. And she didn't want to be nice about it.

The fucking douchebag showed up twenty minutes late and eased into her chair across from me without a hint of an excuse for her tardiness, like I should be waiting with bated breath for her arrival, late or not. She ordered herself a drink by hailing the waitress with a whistle, without bothering to ask if I needed a refill, which was apparent by my empty glass that I did, and then she spent the next thirty minutes boring me with details of her life, her career, and her silver spoon childhood. I toyed with the idea of ordering my own damned drink, then decided against prolonging the agony. Time to call in the troops who, as usual, were only a few booths away watching the slowly sinking ship. Without hesitation, I flipped my hair over my shoulder, which sent the troops into full-blown invade mode.

Why couldn't she say that? Exactly like that? Why did she have to be politically correct without an f-bomb? When she'd agreed to write about her dates in the newspaper column, *The Buddy System,* she'd been duped into thinking she'd have freedom of speech. In her own voice. To show the readers how to use their friends to escape horrible dates.

That obviously wasn't the case. Now she was forced to tone down her anger and disappointment, cut out the sailor tongue, and trim down the past personal experiences that always played into every new date. Wasn't that what this was all about? To help other women, who were also looking for that white picket fence, to stay clear of the assholes, who, unfortunately, sometimes posed as heroes, and who wouldn't help them build that dream?

Yes. That was exactly what Cynthia had said she wanted from Gin. She'd wanted something fresh. Something out of character for a dying column. Yet, every word, every sentence, and every paragraph had been ripped to shreds by the editor and sent back to Gin with blood splatter along with a polite, *This is shit,* message.

"No, ma'am. You cannot use the f-word, or any other clever little wordy dird you seem so fond of. You cannot call people losers because our readers won't relate to the writer's immaturity. Talking about people's wealth, or lack thereof, could turn some readers away. What good would this column or your dating indulgences be if we upset our subscribers? Please revise and send back at your earliest convenience. Sincerely, Patricia."

Gin had resisted driving to the newspaper headquarters to tell Patricia where she could shove the f-bomb. She envisioned a silver-haired woman, plump but not fat, with designer reading glasses with one of those little chain attachments, perched on the end of her nose, wearing a loud flower print dress and flats. Faced with Gin's outburst, her mouth might drop open, and her cheeks would turn a pale pink. The woman probably had never had a lovers' quarrel, let alone indulged in one-night stands. What the fuck did she know about pent-up anger and cheating lovers? If she did, she'd understand and probably snicker at the hostility or overlook a curse word accidentally on purpose dropped into every paragraph.

Patricia's comments and the bloody edits were completely off the mark from what Cynthia had expressed she wanted from Gin.

"I want a little fun set of comical pieces on your dates, the ones that will never amount to anything. Tell the reader how you knew you wouldn't reach second base, why you never wanted to. How you knew this person wasn't the one and why. In other words, how did you conclude that your date was a piece of shit? I want the dirty details. Especially the ones that included your buddies coming to the rescue. I want the reader to relate to every word and wish they had best friends just like yours. Make them jealous of your buddy system."

Maybe Cynthia needed to touch base with her column editor. Clearly, they weren't on the same page.

Gin glanced at the stack of bills just beyond the laptop. Her heart missed a beat. Her desire to keep her grandfather's dream alive—this gas station—was the only reason she'd accepted the offer to write these articles in the first place. Six months. One gig a week. Twenty-six dates total. It seemed a fair amount of attempts to shed some light for others just like herself. Truthfully, some women would always be repeat offenders in their quest for love because they were gluttons for punishment. Or worse, they thought they could tame the tiger. But change them? No way. No matter what she wrote, no matter how detailed she became about spotting the wrong ones, they would never take the advice.

Good thing she couldn't give two shits about them. The little paycheck she got from each article was the only thing that mattered. They were helping her keep the station afloat, although soon, very soon, she was going to sink.

She knew this. Hell! She had tightened her heart around that fact. There was only one way out of this sinkhole. She would have to sell something priceless to save something else just as priceless. She had to sell her grandmother's prized baby. Her beloved Porsche. The very one sitting in her garage that hadn't purred to life in over six months, the very one a collector was itching, begging, patiently waiting, to get his hands on. She'd tinkered, adjusted, replaced parts, but the beautiful beast was just as stubborn as her grandmother had been. And without an engine that would run, that offer would surely be pulled from the table. Soon, she was going to have to bite the bullet and call in the professionals to finish the job. That would cost money she didn't have. Until then, she was going to hold on to her faith that the economy would turn around, that the customers would come back in droves, and she could pull this gas station back to life without selling that beautiful ride. Sad fact was she had a better chance of hitting the lottery and putting an end to her own misery.

The bell chimed, and she glanced out the window to see a brand new powder blue Mazda Miata MX-5 at the gas pump. A young man no older than twenty-five was behind the wheel. An expensive ride for one so young. Probably a gift from Mommy and Daddy for no particular reason at all. Gin could see that the passenger was female and had blond hair.

"Matt! Customer!" Gin yelled for her attendant then realized the sound of the impact wrench had stopped. She hoped he was headed to the pumps.

She glanced back at the words on the screen and tried to find a polite way to restructure them so Patricia wouldn't have to use her bloody ax to shred her voice. There simply wasn't one. The bitch had been disrespectful because that's probably how she'd been raised. A nanny had been her mother figure, the gardener her only true friend, and the chef likely the only person to bake her cookies in the kitchen. Women like her were all the same. Their money, or rather Mommy and Daddy's wallet, was the only backbone they possessed.

A horn blew. Gin glanced out to see a guy with sandy brown hair standing beside his sleek ride. An expectant expression rested on his tanned face.

"Fuck." Gin shoved out of the chair and poked her head in the mechanic bay. The car was still on the lift, and the tires had been changed. "Matt!" When he didn't answer, she huffed and headed for the gas pumps.

No doubt he was behind the station working on that damn flower garden he insisted they needed to liven up the place. No matter how many times he told her he didn't want to run a nursery like his father or take over the family business one day, the more he proved that was exactly what he was destined to do.

Gin pushed out into the sunshine.

The guy quirked an approving brow as she made her way across the asphalt. "Well, hello, beautiful," he cooed.

The passenger turned and focused pale blue eyes on Gin. She rolled her eyes and turned her attention to the radio.

"Fill up?" Gin asked as she moved around the guy and reached for the pump handle.

"Yes, ma'am. I believe all things should be filled up. Filled up tight." He moved beside her as she shoved the nozzle into the tank. He stepped closer. "I could drop the bitch off and come back to show you how full you could get."

She squeezed the handle, popped the lock into place, and turned to face him. Players, two-timing cheaters, plain ole assholes, were the epitome of everything wrong in this world. No one respected love anymore. Hell, no one respected each other.

"Would you like me to clean your windshield?" Gin barked.

"As long as I get to watch." He attempted a sultry wink that resembled a child getting their first taste of a lemon.

With her teeth clenched tight, Gin yanked the squeegee from the soap tray, snapped out a napkin from the holder, and moved to the windshield. His cute date was busy applying a fresh coat of gloss to her lips, focused on her reflection in the side mirror. Ten, twenty years from now, she'd still be with self-centered pricks just like this one. Maybe worse, married to one, stuck at home with two or three kids who were accustomed to Mommy crying in her wine glass and a dad they saw a few hours a week because he was never home before bedtime.

The jerk followed Gin and made a ridiculous lion roar as she stretched out across the hood. "That's it, baby. Make it squeaky clean."

Blondie finally turned her attention to the windshield. She gave a bored smirk. "Are you flirting with a freakin' gas station nobody? She's like, ancient, Thomas."

Thomas belted out an immature cackle.

Gin pushed the pad against the window until trails of water and soap cascaded down the glass then moved back, leaving suds to block the bitch's view. She slowly moved to the side window and leaned down. "Sweetheart, I've been called a lot of things in my lifetime. Ancient isn't among them. Usually, it's God, twisted among the incoherent mumbled erotic cries of women flat on their backs, nipples hard, bodies arched against my face, my tongue dancing—" She abruptly stopped and licked her lips. "Sorry, you're far too young and, without a shadow of a doubt if you date assholes like him, deprived of enough experience to hear the climatic ending to those stories."

The pump popped off, and the girl blinked. She opened her mouth to respond, glanced down at Gin's lips, then moved her attention back to the purse in her lap.

Gin moved away from the window while the jerk began a nerve-splitting laugh, obviously too dumb to realize the joke was on him. She pulled the nozzle free and shoved it back into the pump.

When she turned around, he was standing behind her waving a fifty-dollar bill, no doubt part of his fat weekly allowance, still mentally damaging her with that pathetic smile. She plucked the cash from his grasp and looked down the length of him. "As for your sinfully wicked invitation to be filled up tight, I find that size truly does matter, and according to the flat, practically nonexistent crotch of your chinos, I'd find more pleasure climbing onto the hood of this little boy toy and fucking myself on the hood ornament."

That torturous smile faded from his face.

"Get in the car, Thomas." Blondie popped her head out the window. "We're running late. Your mother will be furious if you miss the golf game again."

Gin winked at her. "Look me up when you get tired of things…" She cut her gaze down to his crotch. "…that can't possibly fill you up."

He narrowed his eyes, then yanked the car door open. He dropped into the seat, revved the engine once, twice, three times, then shoved the shifter into drive. The car lunged forward, then died.

Gin resisted offering her own hysterical laugh as he cranked the engine again and peeled forward, cutting off a minivan on Main Street. The driver promptly laid on the horn.

Her phone rang while she watched the little sports car fade down the street. She glanced at the caller ID before she answered. "Hi, Patrick."

"Hey, doll. Come join me and Steph at the Irish Pub by the interstate in an hour."

Patrick and Steph were her best friends. Her only friends, actually. She'd met them while on a weekend getaway to a gay and lesbian resort and was shocked to learn that they lived less than an hour from each other. Small world, it was. And that they all shared one common factor. They hated boring dates, having to come up with excuses to end a train wreck. So they'd concocted what they called the buddy system over time. They shared each date, even if from afar, and then came to the rescue if the other threw the signal.

At first, it had been rather boring having to suffer through someone else's tedious, going nowhere dates, but as time went on, they created signals and came up with comical ways to end those dead-end dates. Then, the fun had begun.

Gin started walking toward the station. "The one you swore you'd never go back to because there was too much male testosterone and everyone was eyeing the new pretty boy fresh meat because they secretly wanted you?"

"Damn. Did I say that?" He snorted.

"Exactly like that."

"You take everything I say literally, don't you?" He giggled.

"Only so I can use it against you later."

"Well, stop believing everything I say and get your ass over there. I owe you a very belated birthday shot."

"The last time you bought me a birthday drink it came with an escort." Gin walked back inside, saw Matt wasn't in the bay, then turned toward the rear of the building.

"Sweetheart, we did that for your own good. Best friends are obligated to look out for their sexually deprived friends. It's a thing and we must obey the rules of friendship."

Gin rounded the corner and found Matt on his knees, fingers knuckle deep in fertilizer, dark hair splayed against his forehead. She pulled the phone away from her mouth. "Matt, we're closing in ten. Flowers look great. You missed a tip at the pump."

He looked up at her, a puzzled expression washing over his dirt-stained cheeks. "We had a customer?"

"Can you believe it? It's a miracle on Main Street." She rolled her eyes and headed for the office. "As for you, Mr. Patrick, I'll be more than happy to come meet you and Steph for a shot or twelve, but if I so much as sniff your naughty intentions of trying to solve my sexual deprivation problem with yet another hooker, I'm going to seek revenge in the most delicious, wicked way possible."

"Yes, I know, you'll hunt me down and force me to wear that ugly orange garb you call a uniform." He added a "pfft" for good measure.

"No. That's far too easy. I'd prefer to visit that sexy mother of yours the next time your daddy is on a fishing trip. It would be my ultimate honor to teach her how to solve all of my sexual problems. In multiple positions."

Patrick sucked in a dramatic breath. "You would not!"

"If you believe that, then you've never met me. See you in an hour." Gin hung up and plopped down in the chair to stare over the paragraphs one more time.

She was already twelve dates into her twenty-six-date contract, of which only six were due. She was far ahead of the game. But she wanted this particular one off her desktop and winging through cyberspace. That silver-spoon fed twat had been utterly disrespectful. So self-absorbed she had no clue she was doing it. Her kind never had to work for a dollar and never had to earn that respect.

That woman was the total opposite of Gin. She was standing in the very place that had taught her the value of both working for an honest living and earning that respect. From the time she was a tot, she had helped her granddaddy sell bait and tackle to the local fishermen, pumped gas for customers, and used a stepladder to clean the high windows. She'd sat around with the locals and listened to their childhood stories about how curfews were always timed with the streetlights and no one had ever known a spanking quite the likes of a hickory switch. Real life stories that Gin knew nothing about. She'd never had to pick out a switch and she was rarely outside when the streetlights hummed to life because she could normally be found in the gas station.

She could remember their stories vividly, all of them sitting on the porch of the station, spitting their tobacco, retelling the grand ole stories of life.

God, how she missed those guys. Especially her grandparents. They had stepped in without hesitation when her parents were killed in a plane crash on a ten-year anniversary trip to Cancun. They had filled the void and brushed away her tears with loving hugs. They were the root of every loving memory Gin held. Now they were gone. For years, she'd struggled to keep this place afloat in their honor. But the world around her had changed. Malls had been built, chain stores had been erected selling everything, including discounted gas, and the little stores on the outskirts of town were all suffering. Some had already thrown in the towel and sold out to the business moguls steadily making plans to erect industrial complexes.

Gin refused to sell out. Until the county tax assessor slapped a failure to pay property taxes on the front door, until she was legally evicted from the grounds, she'd fight for every single brick. Her granddaddy's sweat and blood were embedded into each layer. Her grandmother's loving hand was in every inch of the layout as well as the antique decorations. She didn't have a choice. She had to fight. For them. For all they had sacrificed to raise her. For them, she had to give it all she had left.

The cursor blinked in the center of the page, silently beckoning her to choose her words wisely. She read the lines once again, editing only a few sentences, which included plucking out the curse words, and before she could change her mind, Gin hit the send button.

"Suck that, Patricia!"

CHAPTER TWO

Carmen Johnson nursed a bottle of beer while Phil yelled at the football game from his stool beside her.

"Another season headed for the shitter. The defense is playing like a bunch of pansies. And that offense? Really? A pack of Little Leaguers could outplay them. How could they expect to make it to the playoffs acting like the Bad News Bears?" Phil jabbed a finger toward the TV on the wall. "Same shit as last year."

Carmen nodded as if she agreed. Phil knew she wasn't into football, although she could throw a mean spiral. Lifting weights, jogging, or long hikes through the woods were more her style. Sweating was her unwinding mechanism. Where the quiet was her only companion. No terrified screams of a child trapped in the back seat of a crushed car. No pleading cries from a mother who couldn't find her child during a fire. No praying that her firemen brothers and sisters would live through the night. No hoping that she would survive her shift.

"Does this mean there won't be any football on Daniel's new big screen for the cookout?" Carmen tossed him a pleading expression.

"Where the hell did you come from?" Phil scoffed. "I've never met a dyke who didn't love football. Someone is going to revoke your card one day. Bet your sweet ass on that."

Carmen shrugged while the front door opened, casting a glow of the streetlights across the room. She turned to see who was entering, hoping, praying, it would be someone who fit the bill for tonight's tasty treat. Sex. She needed sex tonight.

A woman wearing an orange coverall stepped inside. A greasy white ball cap was turned backward on her head hiding the color of her hair. She glanced around the room, gave a quick, uncaring inspection of Carmen, then continued until she found what she was looking for at the pool table and headed in their direction.

Carmen had seen a lot of weirdos come in and out of this bar, but none dressed quite as eccentrically as this one. But curiosity, and the fact that the woman hadn't even so much as checked her out, made her look over her shoulder to follow the woman.

She didn't consider herself hot by any means, but facts were facts. Most women at least gave her a second glance.

The woman joined her friends, a man and a woman, and gave the female an extra long hug. Damn. Taken. Not that she was terribly interested in such bold attire, but it was cool to see the woman didn't care what other people thought of her or their opinion of what she chose to wear.

Clearly, the woman was not the piece of ass Carmen was hoping for because she wasn't a home wrecker, so she turned back to the TV and tried to focus on the radar tucked in the bottom left corner of the screen. Rain was expected for the next few days. Good for her. She was off work and needed to re-energize with some good sleep. Maybe she'd get lucky and find a female to spend a few of those dreary hours with.

Bad for her fellow firefighters, though. Wrecks doubled during heavy rain. Drivers never heeded the "under conditions" change of speed that almost always concluded with a pileup on the freeway.

Someone shrieked behind them.

Carmen and Phil turned to see the guy from the group at the pool table, his mouth agape, and a hand dramatically covering his heart. "You take that shit off your body right this second, missy. I will not stand for this horrendous fashion disaster under my nose."

The woman wearing said getup, the very one who had stepped past Carmen like an afterthought, only offered him a wicked smile. Straight white teeth centered that teasing grin. "This is my 'just in case you decided to add a little extra something-something with my drink' wardrobe. Speaking of which, where is she?" The woman's gaze swept around the room. "I know she's here or you wouldn't have invited me out of the clear blue after ignoring me for weeks now. Someone sexy. Definitely fit. Looking out of place while trying to look like she belongs. Where, oh where, is she?"

The woman continued to look around the room, stalling over each person, until beautiful dark green eyes landed on Carmen once again. This time, her inspection was serious, approving, yet almost comical. That evil smile washed over her lips once again. "Tsk-tsk, Patrick. I warned you. Your mother is going to taste *delicious.*"

She pushed away from the pool table while Patrick yelled after her. "No, Gin. Don't do it!"

Carmen sat frozen in place as the woman walked across the distance, her orange jumpsuit a little too baggy and bunching in all the wrong places, and stepped in between her and Phil. She propped her elbow on the counter and turned her whole body to face Carmen. She smelled like grease and gasoline. Crazy how much she suddenly liked that scent. "Look, sexy, my best friends over there are certifiably insane. I only sign them out of the nuthouse a few hours a week. They're usually harmless, but they tend to have a wicked obsession with my sex life. So, with that said, I'll have to politely decline your sexual services tonight, no matter how tempted I am." She turned her head sideways and casually inspected Carmen. "But I must say, Patrick sure knew what he was doing when he picked you. Kudos to him for knowing my taste in women. I might not make a feast out of his mother, after all."

"Excuse me?" Carmen arched a brow while Phil snickered from behind the woman.

"Don't get me wrong." The woman pushed on. "I'm totally not judging your line of work. To each his own. That's my motto. But it's not for me. Contaminated things tend to gross me out. It's a hereditary germaphobe thing, you see, handed down for generations. I'm not to be blamed for my DNA. Not to mention, I don't share my toys. Never have. I guess I'm still stuck in my terrible twos, never playing nice on the playground, if you know what I mean. With that said, you sharing your, shall we say, dates, with me just won't do."

Carmen couldn't believe what she was hearing. She should correct the woman on her blatant insinuation, all one hundred miles an hour of her, but damn if she wasn't cute trying to explain her way out of a free fuck, paid for kindly by her posse, obviously, who thought this beauty needed a sexual high.

The woman waved her hand in dismissal. "Anyway, I'm sure they rambled on and on, cause they do that sometimes, just ramble on about me being sexually deprived. I'm not. A girl can never be sexually deprived with *Debbie Does Debra* on her laptop and a good vibrator in her nightstand. They mean well, my friends. I love them for their concern. But I must apologize for them having wasted your time. No hard feelings. Good luck with your next customer."

She turned and headed back to her group of friends as Carmen sat dumbfounded by what had just happened. By what she'd just heard. She'd never been mistaken for a hooker before, but suddenly, she would gladly be one for tonight if that's what it took to get that spitfire in her bed.

❖

Steph seized Gin by the arm while Patrick attempted to press himself through the wall, his hand in prayer form against his mouth, making dramatic whimpering sounds. "Tell me you didn't just ask that woman if she was a hooker."

"Of course I didn't."

Patrick let out a breath. "Oh thank you, God!"

Gin smirked. "There was no need to ask. She was shining bright like a diamond. I could have picked her out of a crowd of a thousand looking all suave and in charge on her stool, nursing the same beer from the minute I walked in, sexy as sin in her fake fireman T-shirt. Good try, you two. Good try, indeed." She blew a kiss toward Patrick who looked nauseated.

"I'm utterly mortified," he mumbled. "She *is* a fireman, you ding-a-ling!"

Steph crossed her arms with a nod. "Yes, dumbass. She's a real fireman."

Gin looked between Steph and Patrick and saw the truth in their eyes.

Fuck!

She slowly turned back to the woman and found her watching, a grin on her face. The cutie held up her beer and cheered the air before turning her attention back to the game on the TV.

A dyke, perched on a stool, in a bar, right in view of the front door so she could snatch the best options, glued to football. What were the odds? Like one out of one! Duh. Could these sexy butches be any more original? They were all the same. Right down to needing those notches on their bedposts.

Nothing aggravated Gin more than watching a woman wait for a piece of ass to jump in her lap. Even worse, the woman was a fucking hero. Those were the absolute worst.

"Even better!" Gin sighed. "You know my stance on women in uniform."

"Okay, take a breath, everyone. Let's be calm about this." Patrick moved to the pool table. "Breathe, Patrick. Breathe. Let's just act normal. Like we have the good sense God gave us." He leaned awkwardly against the table and crossed his ankles, a poor attempt to appear casual. The action twisted his balance, and he slid sideways for a second before he stumbled and caught himself. "Shit!"

"Calm down, spazoid. She's a fireman, not an assassin." Gin moved to the pool table. "Let's play. And where's my drink you promised?"

"Not until you remove this disgrace for clothing." Patrick swung his fist on his hip and stared her down, forgetting he was mortified only seconds before.

"Fine." Gin snagged the cap off her head and let her hair spill out from beneath.

She couldn't help but glance toward the hottie she'd just called a whore. The woman was watching. Her eyes admiring and curious.

Gin despised the heated expression on the fireman's face. She was cute, yet expectant from the way she'd just turned her attention on Gin. That's the way they worked. The heroes. A move, a wink, a mastered expression. They were good at it. It sucked that the woman wore a uniform for a living. Not just any uniform. One that screamed she was a hero.

Gin had been played far too hard by a hero. Women who were supposed to be protectors, who used their skills for their own wicked benefits. They were disgusting.

Teresa had been the worst of them all. A cop. A good cop. Tall, fit, and all gentleman. Gin had seen her future in those blue eyes. Saw them living a happy, simple life. A home they could be proud of. Until she'd caught her, in uniform, fucking one of the tellers from the local bank on her lunch break, in her patrol car, in the back of a twenty-four-hour burger joint parking lot.

A woman who was supposed to protect her had broken her. The person who had sworn she would always be loyal took unloyalty to epic proportions. The woman who had promised her forever had called time's up. And the woman who had vowed that Gin held her heart, had ripped hers right down the center.

Years had now passed, but Gin would always remember how dirty she felt while she stood beside the car. Questions had rung through her mind as she stepped to the driver's door, calculating the dramatic bloodshed outcome of the moment. How long had the affair been going on? Was it an affair? Or was she one of many? Was this the first time? Would it ever happen again? Did it matter?

No. It didn't matter. Nothing the classless hero could have said or done or begged her way out of would have changed a damn thing. And it sure as hell wouldn't change the pain the vision of her lips locked on another female had already caused. The damage had been done. Could never be undone.

Anger had bubbled hard and fast as she took several steps back away from the cruiser. Then she took another step, swallowing down the lump threatening to dislodge itself and send tears streaming down her face. She did not cry. Not then. Not the next day. Not ever. The image before her, her lover's hands, her fiancée's fingers, playing down the pants of the bank teller's, ensured she had been saved from a life of cheating habits. If she could have found her breath, she would have thanked her.

As quickly as she could, she'd darted inside the restaurant, ordered a black coffee, which Teresa didn't drink, and asked the cashier to deliver it to the patrol car. The girl even smiled at the opportunity to serve a cop. The embarrassment Teresa and her fuck partner would be faced with was enough to make Gin smile as she turned back toward the exit door.

When she walked out, she knew she'd never look back. Never again. She didn't care if a woman drove a trash truck or milked cows on a farm or even flipped burgers to pay the rent, she'd fall for anyone, but never again would it be for someone in hero's attire.

Not even if they looked quite as delicious as this one.

To give this hottie a taste of what she would never have, Gin slowly unzipped the coverall and pushed it off her shoulders. She held that smoldering stare and pushed the material down her torso, over her hips, and down her legs.

The woman never looked away.

Gin kicked out of the coverall and moved her attention back to the pool table. Enough. She was here to enjoy a beer with her friends, not toy with a player.

Twenty minutes later, they were well into a conversation about financial woes, her grandmother's car, and the possibility of losing her business. Or rather, being forced to sell it to save her own ass.

"I've told you over and over to call my brother to help you fix the car," Steph said as she shot a solid ball into the corner pocket.

"The same brother that poured two quarts of water into his motor a month ago?" Gin moved to the opposite side of the table when Steph missed her next shot.

"Hey, how was he supposed to know those precious nephews of mine had taken the bottles from the trash and refilled them with water?" Steph protested.

"Did the clear liquid not give him a clue?" Gin giggled. "But on a more serious note, I need a specialist. Someone who deals with classics."

"It's a car, Gin. Don't they all operate the same?"

"Heads up, ladies. We have company approaching," Patrick announced.

Gin glanced up over her stick to see the hottie from the stool and her sidekick coming to a stop near the table. She took her shot and watched a stripe drop into the side pocket before she stood to face them.

"I heard you guys talking about cars, one of my favorite subjects, and couldn't resist being nosy. I'm Phil." He glanced at Steph and offered a sweet smile. "My non-talking, non-escort friend here is Carmen. We're just plain ole firemen." He nodded toward Gin as if that cleared up her confusion. It definitely did. His buddy was a tool. Not just a possibility of being a tool.

Carmen tipped her head. "Sorry to disappoint you."

"Me, too. I liked you better as a hooker." Gin turned back to the game, found her shot, and bent over the table. "I absolutely despise firemen."

Chapter Three

Another stripe dropped into the corner pocket, and Gin stalled to rechalk her cue stick, wishing the firemen would walk their asses back to the stools they came from. No one spoke while she moved to the opposite side of the table, entirely too close to Carmen. She smelled good. If only she weren't a fireman. If only she hadn't been perched on a bar stool waiting for a piece of ass to bump into her. Gin could definitely envision a night of raw sex with her. It would be good. She could tell. But the fact still remained. She was the dirty devil wrapped in a hero's T-shirt.

"I see no one is going to breathe while you prowl those shiny balls. Should make a great addition to your next article. How ever will you write yourself as the woman who called a fireman a hooker?" Patrick gave a nervous laugh, still clearly affected by Gin's bravery.

"This isn't a real date, so no use wasting time with a keyboard. Besides, you know I would never date a fireman." Gin bumped another stripe into the side pocket and glanced up at Carmen. "Ever."

Carmen shifted from one foot to the other, then took a sip of her beer.

"You're a writer?" Phil asked.

Gin opened her mouth to answer when Patrick blurted, "Hell yes, she is. She writes all the dos and don'ts of dating in the local newspaper."

Phil widened his eyes. "Wait, you're Virginia? The Buddy System author?"

"The one and only," Patrick cooed.

Gin gave him a death stare, and he cleared his throat and looked away.

"That shit is real? Like, real dates?" Phil asked.

"Unfortunately." Gin struck the ball and missed the pocket.

Steph moved around the table with Phil admiring every step.

"The taxidermist who brought you a stuffed rat? Real?" Phil arched a brow.

"Real. I can't make that shit up."

"So the buddy system is a real thing?" Phil looked back to Steph. "You're Sharonda?"

Steph batted her lashes and gave a mini curtsy. "In the flesh." She pointed toward Patrick. "He's Bartholomew. And Gin, of course, as Virginia. We are the three amigos." She pressed her index finger against her lips. "Shh. Secrets shared in Delaney's should remain in Delaney's."

Phil looked amazed as he glanced between the three of them. "Absolutely awesome. I'm addicted to the column. It's funny as hell."

"Well, don't get too attached. My contract runs out in twelve more dates, and I'll be hanging up the glass slippers. Cinderella isn't going to find Princess Charming in this sea of losers."

"You date for a paycheck?" Carmen finally spoke.

Gin glanced down her body. Fit as hell. From her flat belly that looked hard as stone, down to her athletic thighs encased in her faded jeans. Absolutely delicious. Why did she have to be a hero?

"You would prefer me to fuck for one?" Gin asked.

A sexy smile lifted the corners of Carmen's lips. "Depends on your fee."

Phil interrupted the trance by nudging Carmen. "Steph, I mean, *Sharonda*, busted up a date by pretending to be a jealous ex-lover, crying like a toddler, begging for a second chance, wiping her nose all over the date's sleeve. I've never laughed so hard."

Steph huffed a breath against her nails and polished them across her T-shirt. "That was one of my better moments if I do have to say so myself. Oscar performance, it was. Poor woman didn't know whether to hug me or call the cops."

"So how, exactly, does this buddy system work?" Carmen asked and watched as Gin bent over the table to line up her next shot.

She wanted Gin. Beneath her. Above her. In her. And she wanted her now. Especially since Gin was so verbal about her dislike of her. She wanted nothing to do with Carmen. It made the game so much sweeter.

Gin looked up over her stick. "Pay attention, stud. It's already begun."

Everyone went quiet again while Gin tapped the corner pocket, lined up her shot, and dropped the eight ball in for the win.

Carmen couldn't tell if Gin was serious or full of shit. Either way, she started looking for clues or signs, maybe even extra language tossed in. She was curious to discover how these three amigos managed to signal each other without anyone being the wiser.

"I'm out," Steph announced. "Patrick, she's all yours." She held the stick out to him.

"She threatened to make my mother a carpet muncher. Nuh-uh. She's evil." Patrick waved the stick away and took a sip of his drink.

Carmen took the stick from Steph. "I'll play her."

Gin perched herself against the table. "You have nothing to wager that I would be interested in."

"Sure I do. We'll make it a mystery prize." She plucked a napkin off the bar, the chalk off the table, then tore the paper in half and handed it to Gin. "Write down your bet and lay it on the table. Winner reveals. Every ball dropped is another question asked. Since I'm pretty handy with a stick, you can tell me more about this buddy system. Deal?"

Gin studied her. Patrick was right. She was seriously sexually deprived because the longer Carmen stared at her with those hard brown eyes, the more she wanted to fuck her.

God knew she'd rather swim in a cesspool of man-eating sharks, while on the rag, than let another hero touch her. So what was it about this particular one that piqued her wet need?

No matter. Just a few more minutes of this electric energy and she could call it a night. She had dates to line up. Another article to write. Another *You did it again, Gin,* email to read from Patricia.

"Deal," Gin said.

They both wrote their bet on their napkins, laid them face down on the table, and then Carmen racked the balls. She stuck the tray beneath the table and waved for Gin to begin. "Ladies first."

Gin chalked her stick. "That was your first and final mistake." She broke the stack. Balls scattered in all directions. A solid fell into the far corner pocket.

"Lucky break. Ask away," Carmen stated proudly.

Gin moved around the table. "I don't have any questions. I know all I need to know about you."

"You think you do. But you don't."

Gin found her shot, bent over, and struck another ball in. "I know enough."

"Like what?"

Once again, Gin moved around the table. She rechalked, lined up another shot, and bent over, fully aware that Carmen was following her every move. "That stool at the end of the bar is your designated spot." She tapped another ball in. "No one ever sits in it. Like they know it's Carmen's chair. The fireman's. The hero's throne."

Gin glanced up and found Carmen staring down at her. Carmen offered no response.

"You sit in that particular chair because you need the view of the front door. You need to see who walks through it." Gin bent over and struck another ball in. "You need first dibs on fresh meat. You prefer first-time fucks over repeats. They're more exciting. Makes for better sport, to catch fresh prey."

Carmen glanced toward the stool in question. Of course that was true. Was she that apparent? Was that so horrible? It sucked that Gin knew it. Not that Gin knew it, but that it was true.

Gin continued to the opposite side of the table and paused to rechalk. "You wear that T-shirt because it scores the pussy for you. You never even have to leave your chair. The women flock to heroes, don't they, Carmen?" She laid the chalk down and bent over the table.

"Not always." But Carmen knew that was a lie. Almost always.

Another ball fell into the corner pocket. Carmen shifted from one foot to the other.

Gin continued. "You never actually date people. No candlelit dinners. No holding hands on a lazy stroll through the park. No fright night movies and popcorn and cuddles when the scary part flashes on the screen. Nope. Not for Carmen. That's not her style, is it?" Gin tapped another ball in and rose. "You just fuck them. Maybe multiple times when this bar offers slim pickings. But you're gentleman enough to make sure the rules are clear. That they get only one shot with you. Because that's what heroes do. They protect people. And you think fucking women who know they won't get to wake up in your bed, is heroic. Makes you feel good about yourself."

Carmen shifted once again. This game was all but over, and she was no closer to getting to know Gin than she was before she stepped a foot inside the bar. It appeared Gin knew far too much about her.

This charade wasn't going to end well for her if she didn't get back in control. She lifted her chin as Gin took in a breath before speaking again.

"I know so much about you, stud, that I know exactly what you wrote on your napkin."

Carmen was almost afraid to ask, but curiosity got the better of her. "Oh yeah? What was my wish?"

Gin laid the stick across the table and slowly walked toward Carmen, that green gaze flicking like the northern nights. "The only thing a player would ever want. The one and only thing to kick-start the end of her night where the *real* prize awaits. A kiss. You wanted a kiss. Because that's how it all begins, doesn't it, Carmen?" Gin moved closer.

Carmen was speechless. How the hell did she know that? How was she so transparent and why did it make her feel dirty?

"All you had to do was ask. This game, this pretend to get to know me bullshit, was redundant." Gin teasingly ran her tongue along her front teeth. "I guess when the prey doesn't run, the game isn't as sweet, huh?"

Before Carmen could change her mind, before Gin could change hers, she took control and stepped into Gin. She captured those lips with a rushed groan.

Patrick let out a sharp exhale of breath, but everything else around them was deathly quiet. The chatter from nearby tables. The music from the jukebox spilling through the speakers. The rattle of glasses from behind the counter. Everything. Vanished.

Gin was shocked into expelling a sigh as Carmen's tongue swam against her own. It was like heaven and sin in her mouth. Her stomach knotted as the kiss deepened and her insides tightened as she leaned heavily into Carmen.

The rush of warmth spread down her limbs as Carmen pulled her closer. She was hot. Fit. No doubt she would make her fantasies burst to life in bed.

If only she wasn't the devil behind the hero's logo. She stood for everything Gin despised. Everything that had caused her undue pain. Everything that had given her the material to build this brick wall around herself.

She allowed herself a few more seconds of this awakening kiss, her insides cramped tight, her body electrified, and finally, slowly, with a little more regret than she knew she could still possess for women like Carmen, she wrapped one arm around Carmen's neck and wove her fingers through that unkempt hair.

The buddy system was triggered. For a split second, she thought about adding the other arm. For sure, Patrick was holding his breath for that exact move. He was determined to marry off his best friend. His sexually deprived best friend. That very move would call off the amigos' next set of actions.

Problem was, she couldn't be a repeat offender no matter how sinfully hot this kiss felt. No matter how many times her insides flamed to life, she couldn't forget all the hard lessons she'd endured at the hands of a woman just like this one. She never wanted to forget that pain. Or the humiliation.

Five seconds, ten. Her body hummed as Carmen wrapped an arm around her waist and tucked her in even tighter against her body. Gin could feel the heat from her. From her very tight, hard body. She wanted to grind against her. Wanted to hike her leg up and over her hip and invite Carmen to drive against her. The need was almost overpowering her common sense.

Twenty seconds. Regretfully, thankfully, time was up.

"Gin, I hate to interrupt your need-a-room moment, but your dad is on the phone. Said it was urgent," Steph interrupted, dead on time.

Gin pulled slowly out of the kiss and looked up into those eyes. There was nothing smug in them. She'd expected smug. Carmen had gotten her wish without winning the game. However, she could never win the prize. If it cost her dying breath, she could never be a notch on this hottie's bedpost. Oh, but she could visualize. For sure, she would.

"I need to take this." Gin lowered her voice into a sultry whisper. "Wait for me here?" She fingered the fire station logo on Carmen's T-shirt and felt the hardness beneath the touch.

Did she have to be so fit? So lean? Maybe Patrick was right about her sexual deprivation. For sure her night was going to end with wicked thoughts on her mind while the vibrator hummed between her thighs.

"Of course," Carmen replied, staring down on Gin's lips.

Gin stepped out of Carmen's embrace, took the phone from Steph, and pressed it against her ear while she turned toward the front door. "Hi, Dad. What's wrong?"

Carmen watched her retreating steps until she slipped out the front door, her crotch a throbbing wet mess. Of course she had reactions to women. Who wouldn't? She was horny. Single. No attachments and no baggage. She was free to react any way she wanted with any female she wanted. But not like this. Not from a single kiss. Especially from a woman who couldn't stand her for following a dream. A destination.

She prayed the phone call wouldn't keep Gin too long. It was time to take this fireman-hater to bed. Time to conquer this quest.

When she turned around, she found Steph smiling at her. Patrick didn't look so happy. Something in those expressions made her stomach tighten.

She spotted Gin's napkin on the edge of the table and picked it up.

You blinked and missed it, handsome. That's how the buddy system works, the napkin said.

Carmen had been duped.

She glanced back at the door, then to Steph, wondering how she'd missed the signal that would send one of the two amigos into action. "She's not coming back, is she?"

CHAPTER FOUR

Carmen stepped out of the shower to the faint sounds of laughter drifting down the hall from the day room.

By the loud hoorahs and clapping and cheerful bellows, the foosball game was a tight one.

She stepped in front of the mirror and used her towel to wipe the fog away. A tired expression stared back at her. The little crow's feet in the corners of her eyes looked deeper, more distinguished. There were permanent "weight of the world" lines on her forehead. Or that's what she preferred to call them. Wrinkles sounded too old. Thirty-six wasn't old, dammit.

She sighed and widened her eyes, trying to smooth the corner lines, creasing the wrinkles, yes, they were wrinkles, along her forehead even deeper. The hectic day was to blame for her fatigue and forlorn emotion. Her shift had been active, starting at a convenience store with a terrified mother whose little boy had locked the car doors while Mom filled up with gas. Thankfully, the morning had been comfortable with fall temperatures, and they'd been able to take their time coaxing little Jeremy into pressing the unlock button while bribing him with suckers and stuffed animals.

She'd felt sorry for the mother who had shed tears the entire time and practically squeezed the life out of him as soon as the door opened and swore she was never leaving her keys in the car again, even if she was only three feet away. Of course, like any other toddler, he'd been oblivious to Mom's panicked affection, more interested in the fuzzy bunny, lollipop, and plastic fireman's hat they kept stocked on the truck for such scenarios.

It was days like today when she was reminded that she'd once wanted those things in her life. Kids. A spouse. The normal white picket dream. Although she'd never truly desired them. It was simply the way of the world. It's what everyone wanted, deep down. To get married, reproduce, raise those children to be productive members of society, etcetera, etcetera.

She couldn't, and shouldn't, desire those things. Her life, her career, promised that whoever that significant other was would be heartbroken and left alone to hold the reins. Just like her great-grandmother. Just like her grandmother. Just like her mother. Her family's curse ensured she, too, would die in the line of duty. A plaque with her picture would adorn the firehouse walls, as well as Delaney's, along with the rest who had given their lives to save another. That was her destiny, and she'd settled into the fact that sooner or later, the curse would come to take her, too.

But unlike the men from her family tree, Carmen would never leave behind a widow. Her mother and grandmother had mourned for far too long. She could never inflict that kind of pain and emptiness on another.

Nor could she give up her dream. Her only dream. A dream that was hers long before she knew what wishes and desires truly were. She loved and adored and lived for her job. It was in her blood. Handed down for many generations. Like it, hate it, it was all she knew. It was all she would ever know. Work. Women. Always and forever in that exact order. Until it was her time to be plucked from existence.

A loud clap of laughter echoed down the hall and snapped Carmen from her thoughts.

Yes. Work. Women. That was how she lived her life, even if events like today made her ache for what she could never have. What she shouldn't, mustn't, want.

Fifteen minutes later, she entered the day room to watch the finale. These guys were her brothers. Her sisters. She loved them. Protected them. They were her family, all the family outside her biological family that she would ever have, and that was okay. She couldn't go wrong with people who would always have her back in the same way she had theirs.

"So, blue balls, huh?" Daniel scooted in beside her, lollipop in hand. "I hear some beauty left my girl hanging like a limp wrist. I never dreamed a day would come that you, the stud of dyke land, would get the shaft. Did it hurt? Was there grease involved? At least a little reach around foreplay before she stuck that boot up your ass?" His serious expression finally faded, and he laughed.

Carmen cut her sights on Phil who looked the other way. "Big mouth."

Yes. That had happened. She'd been teased, yet not teased, then left standing in her own wet heat. Nothing else had been on her mind since. That kiss. Hot. Sinfully hot. The need had slowly turned to an ache. Now it was something far worse. An aching want. She wanted to pick up exactly where they'd left off. Sex. Sex had never been so needed. She wouldn't be satisfied until Gin was screaming against her tongue.

"That's a story to go down in history," Phil teased her. "What kind of team player would I be if I didn't share that story with our firehouse family? The night Carmen was turned down. Epic."

"The month is young, asshole. I still have time for the kill," Carmen said. But something deep down told her it wouldn't be that simple.

Gin was going to be work. Work she was prepared to do.

"That book is closed, sister. She can't stand you." Phil snickered like he was visually playing out the scene in his head. "She kissed your ass good-bye. Literally. While you stood there with your tongue practically dragging on the floor behind her. Waiting like a good little submissive."

"What I wouldn't give to have been there watching our girl turning blue," Daniel said then pushed the sucker back in his mouth for a second. "Was it like puppy love and Cupid's arrow and shit? Did you cry?"

"Shut up, manchild." Carmen shouldered him.

"Worse," Phil injected. "She was glued to that very spot. Didn't move a muscle because the sexy lady said *Wait for me here?*" Phil ended with a high-pitched tone, mocking Gin. "And her amigos were grinning like demented fools behind her while she was held spellbound by that tight ass walking away. Hot, man. I'm telling you, she was fucking hot. And that woman was an ice princess for our queen here. Cold. Calculated. It was fucking awesome!"

"I miss all the good shit!" Daniel stuffed the lollipop back in his mouth then moved to the table to watch Robert and William dominate the game. "I spent the weekend painting my daughter's room pink. Pink, goddammit. Not just any pink. Bubblegum pink. Beth was happy though. I really like it when Beth is happy." He wiggled his eyebrow.

Carmen admired that he and his wife were still crazy in love after so many years. They'd shared buying a new house, adding decor to their yard, adding a kid, all among the fears of kissing her husband good-bye every time he left for his shift. How did she do it? How did any of them do it?

"You love it and you know it," Robert said as he jerked on the handles and missed the ball.

William quickly twirled his handle, knocking the ball into the slot, and then roared with the victory, arms fisted toward the ceiling like Rocky Balboa.

"Fucker! You cheated!" Robert slapped a twenty on the table and turned to Phil. He squeezed his shoulder and shook him a few times. "And what about our boy here? Snagged himself a girl's phone number? Say it ain't so."

"Yep, that he did," Carmen said. She'd heard all about it, how they'd talked on the phone for six hours about absolutely nothing, yet everything. That Steph was a medical receptionist at the local hospital, had a German shepherd that said "mama" for treats, and who was helping Patrick get settled into his new apartment in town, and loved painting.

Carmen couldn't remember the last time Phil had been so doe-eyed over a woman. Years, for sure. He was too nice. Women didn't like the too nice type. They wanted a knight in shining armor. They wanted a hero. They wanted someone with a backbone. Phil was a hero with a backbone. Just a super nice one. It was possibly his only downfall when it came to women. She knew a special kind of woman would come along and laugh at all of his crappy jokes.

"What are you gonna do without your boy? He'll be whistling the wedding song in no time, spitting out babies, and painting bedrooms bubblegum pink." Daniel clapped him on the back. "Little Phil, joining the rest of the hitched world. Who would have ever thunk it?"

"He's going to make a pretty bride," Robert cooed.

They joshed each other for another hour then Carmen grabbed her duffel bag and headed out. She was starving. A quick stop for takeout, a ten-minute drop-in at the bar, mainly to see if Gin would make another appearance, which was doubtful since she hadn't in the last two weeks. Yes. She'd checked. It was stupid, but it got under her skin how much Gin hated her. How she'd left her waiting, looking like an idiot.

The experience was making her feel uncomfortable. If only she knew why. If only she knew how. She didn't get feelings where women were concerned. There was never a need to.

She drove the few miles to the restaurant, images of green eyes dancing in her view, decided she wouldn't go by the bar, because, why should she? Never, ever did she chase women. Yet, for weeks, she'd been looking for one. She needed to get her head screwed back on straight and get herself back in check. Work. Women. In that damn order.

With determination that she would push this woman out of her mind, Carmen parked the car and headed inside the restaurant.

❖

Gin stared across the table at her third date in two weeks. The woman's lips were moving, but all she heard was blah, blah, blah. She hadn't been listening since the woman bragged about her collection of rare coins, how she'd been a collector since she was a tot, because her granddaddy taught her how to spot the rarest ones, and then proceeded to show Gin pictures of all her precious dogs captured lovingly on her phone, complete with those little fucking hearts and lips. *Head thump.*

Dear Lord, forgive her, but who the fuck cared? Coins? Dogs? Really? Is this what her dating life, her sex life, had regressed into? Listening to sexy butch women talk about their beloved animals? How, why, did animals and women begin to equate to a gay thing? Seriously. How did the two begin to go hand in hand? If you saw a gay person, you saw a freaking dog. And almost certainly, it would be some ankle biter breed.

If it wouldn't be completely rude to bang her head repeatedly on the table, she would. Why, oh why, had she traded her pajamas for this cute sundress tonight? Why hadn't she just left the emails alone? Why, fucking why, did she have to respond to Laura's ping on Match-Us inviting her for dinner tonight?

She knew why. Because deep down she was determined to find her equal. As sick as the search was becoming, as boring as it sometimes became, she wanted that connection so bad. She wanted what Steph had finally found. That spontaneous combustion.

Yes, Steph. The best friend who was missing from this equation tonight because she wanted to spend more time with Phil at one of the firemen's houses to watch football. Like she hadn't spent almost every night with him for the past week.

"He's the most adorable thing ever. He brought me a rose, Gin. For no reason. A single, beautiful, perfect red rose," Steph had said, that little squeal and giggle in her voice that said she was head over heels.

Normally, Gin wouldn't hesitate to voice her opinion. *You're moving too fast. Slow down.* But not this time. This time, she could hear the jealousy in her thoughts. She wanted that. She wanted to giggle. She wanted to squeal. She wanted that fucking rose. For no damn reason. She wanted to grin from a text. She wanted to get wet from a memory.

Was that too much to ask? Was that asking the world the unthinkable? For herself, obviously, the desire was out of the question. This is what the world gave her. Women who collected coins and took a billion pics of their tiny fucking dogs.

Maybe she was cursed. Cursed to live alone forever. Maybe the single womanizing players had the answer the whole time. Fuck them, let them know all you're going to do is fuck them, then move on through life like you never knew each other.

Seemed simple enough. Easy enough. Yet, that's not how she wanted to live life. She wanted an equal. Someone to put her in her place when she was upset about something ridiculous. Someone who wouldn't hesitate to push her through the bedroom door when her temper was blown and her sharp tongue was out of control.

Ah. Yes. Hot, makeup sex. She wanted a whole lot of that.

"My mother is going to Italy next month for some long overdue shopping. My mother loves shopping. While there, she's going to visit the local animal rescue facilities in hopes of adding another little furbaby to our family. Although, if you can imagine, they have the most insane adoption rules. She'll have to wave her magic wand, like always."

Gin blinked out of her thoughts and resisted pushing away from the table. No. That's not what she wanted to do. She wanted to climb onto this table, prowl across the top like a naughty girl, open her legs in a very unladylike position, grab Laura by that stylish flip haircut, and shove her face first against her crotch, just to watch her eyes widen by such bold behavior. God knew the women Laura's nose to the sky family expected her to date, especially her wand-wielding mother, would be mature, classy, put together, and never behave badly. Gin wanted to behave badly in honor of this nuclear disaster.

This had gone on too long. Free dinner or not, this was insane. No woman should have to endure such boredom. She could very well be coming over her vibrator right now instead of inflicting this mental anguish upon herself. How many more of these dates would she have to endure? How many, beyond this contract, would it take to find the one who stirred slick heat between her thighs?

Movement caught her attention, and she turned to see Carmen, the non-hooker, whose kiss had stirred that very slick heat, stepping through the front door wearing a pair of loose fitting jeans and a faded gray T-shirt with the firehouse logo in dark blue. She'd left Carmen waiting for her, lust filling those pretty brown eyes. That had been the best. Knowing that she'd gotten to Carmen, that she'd gotten under her skin, that she'd had her dangling, horny, and positive she was going to take Gin home.

No such luck for the pussy collector. But damn if she hadn't thought about what their night could have been like ever since. Raw, unadulterated sex is what it would have been. It sucked so bad that she knew it, that she'd rejected it, and that she was still thinking about what could have been.

Carmen took a bag from the cashier, then turned and captured Gin in those dark eyes. An amused smile slipped across her lips as she looked between Gin and her date.

With that smile widening, she headed toward their table. Heat stirred with every step, and Gin's stomach knotted. A butterfly fluttered in her gut.

Carmen stopped at the table. "Gin, right?"

"As if you could ever forget my name." Gin winked. Of course this bitch remembered her name. A woman like Carmen wouldn't forget it. The notches on her bedpost, she'd forget. But not the one who got away.

"Ever get that car fixed?" Carmen asked, dodging another fact.

"No, I didn't."

Carmen glanced toward the date. "I'm assuming you're not a mechanic?"

Laura straightened. "No. Can't say that I am. Never been handy with a wrench. I prefer to hire those who are," she said defiantly, obviously threatened by the sight of a woman who clearly wasn't afraid of power tools.

Carmen leaned down. "Speaking from experience, insist that Gin pay you in advance for your sexual favors. She has a nasty habit of stiffing the working girls, if you know what I mean." She stood to full height and trapped Gin in another scalding stare. "And teasing. She's very, very good at teasing."

Gin uncrossed her legs and slowly recrossed over the opposite leg to ease the burn. Carmen was entirely too sexy. And those eyes. Devouring her. Making promises that a woman who knew she was truly hated should never make.

"You asked for a demonstration. I obliged."

The smile on Carmen's face held Gin captivated. Raw sex stood behind that smile. Her crotch burned from the images. Would sex with a hero again be so bad? She could leave her morals in the car to pick up the following day on her way to work. Seemed to work for most of the world, why not her?

"True. I did, didn't I? Trust that I have every intention of finishing exactly where that demonstration left off." Carmen shook out of the stare as if it took genuine effort and turned back to Laura. "Sorry to have interrupted her thirteenth, or more, date, in the past few weeks. It would have been rude to pass by without saying hello. I detest rude people. Don't you agree?"

Laura awkwardly held out her hand. "Speaking of manners, I'm Laura. It's great to meet you."

Carmen looked down at the offered hand. "No need for such formalities. The next time I see Gin, I won't see you. That's her style."

Gin squeezed her legs together as the heat gathered. Maybe she could just leave her morals at the station. She could pick them back up after she wrote a detailed article about tonight's adventure. "Not always. I might not play well with others, but I actually like some people. Just not you."

Carmen took a step back. "Be sure to tip your local hooker this time, Gin. She has wrench wielders to pay for. Have a great night, you two."

Laura gasped, clearly undecided whether to chase after Carmen, which wouldn't end well for someone clearly not accustomed to physically standing up for herself, let alone her date, or to laugh at a joke she wasn't sure was a joke. The indecision on her face almost made Gin laugh out loud.

She couldn't help but smile as she watched Carmen push out into the setting sun. Oh, how she loved a smartass. Someone who wouldn't take her shit, who would give it right back, then fuck her into complete silence. If only that kind of control freak didn't have a hero's logo attached to her uniform. Damn, it sucked so bad that she would have to put that vibrator to use again tonight.

"Did that woman just assume I was a hooker?" Laura panted. "Thirteenth date? What did she mean by that? Is this a habit?"

Just like that, the date was over. The buddy system clearly wasn't required.

Chapter Five

W"hen are you gonna sell this baby to me?" Daniel kicked the passenger front tire of Carmen's '68 Camaro as she tossed her duffel bag into the trunk, eager to officially end another long and tiresome shift.

A fire had kick-started her day. One that could have very well gotten out of control had someone driving down the interstate not seen the smoke. By the time they arrived on the scene, the brush fire had spread deep into the foliage and thankfully was cornered by a two-lane frontage road. Another teen? She hoped. But something in her gut told her it was far worse. The fires were happening too often. They were too random. Too out of sequence. Something was amiss, and she prayed the investigators were on top of the matter.

That call had ended with another one close behind. A wreck on the freeway not two miles ahead that caused a six-car pileup and backed up traffic for ten miles during lunch rush hour. Thankfully, no one had lost their life because a woman found it necessary to text her husband back about dinner plans. It wasn't just the teens acting like idiots lately. Seemed no one could wait to get to a safe location then stop to check their electronic devices.

Didn't they value their lives? Other people's lives? Didn't they value their families? Wasn't it important to make it home safely? The answer was an obvious no. Not lately, anyway. Six months ago, they had been called to a fatal crash from someone texting. Another, two months before that. Same scenario.

Her job was to pick up the pieces. To cover their bodies from public viewers. To clean up the mess, pack up their gear, and head back to the station. Yet it seemed she left a little piece of herself at every fatality.

Sooner or later, she was going to feel nothing. There wouldn't be anything left to leave behind. Wasn't she already moving in that direction? It seemed every death got a little bit easier. She wasn't sure how she felt about that. It was one thing to be good at her job. Quite another not to feel a damn thing.

"Beth would have your dick on a chopping block and my head on a silver platter if we ever shook on that deal." Carmen closed the lid, walked to the driver's door, and crossed her arms over the roof. Fatigue settled in her shoulders. "I kind of like my head right where it is."

Daniel bowed his chest out and posed. "I'm not afraid of her. She doesn't scare me one bit."

Carmen snickered. "Yes, the hell she does. She has the key to the bedroom door." She threw a wink his way. "Go home, leash boy."

Daniel deflated himself with a huff and opened his car door. "Well, at least I have the coolest doghouse this side of South Carolina. How many other pussy-whipped people do you know who can say that?" He wagged a finger at her.

"You're the man, Daniel." Carmen dropped into the seat, thankful rest was close on the agenda. She needed to recharge the batteries, reboot with some beauty sleep. Maybe after some much-needed sleep, she'd feel more like herself again. Right now, she was dog tired.

She revved the car to life and felt the tension bundle in her back.

The week had been total chaos. A brush fire, an abandoned building fire, as well as a car fire. Were the teens in full swing again? It wouldn't be the first time the pranksters had gotten out of control. She hoped that wasn't the case once again. It would be a shame to have another arsonist on their hands like the one from five years ago. The man, heartbroken from a recent divorce and with nothing else to live for, so he claimed, had burned down several abandoned buildings, ending with his own house, before they caught him. It had been Carmen's first taste of investigating fires instead of fighting them. She'd never admitted that her curiosity still remained for that field. It was far less dangerous. More interesting, too.

Carmen shook off the thoughts. No one in her family had ever stepped out of the firemen's boots. The men in her family chain were beasts. Unafraid. Heroes. She would be the same. Was being the same.

Food. She just needed some food at her favorite mom-and-pop restaurant, a little shut-eye, and she'd be good as new. Tomorrow, she was going to shake herself back into form.

In the distance, she spotted a thin plume of black smoke. Probably a backyard fire, but the firefighter in her couldn't ignore the possibility of something worse. It would eat her alive if the headlines in tomorrow's news proved she'd ignored an emergency.

So she cut down a few back roads until she found the source. Just someone burning leaves in a metal barrel. All legal. All under the supervision of the homeowners.

With her instincts back in check, she headed toward Main Street when she spotted a woman on a ladder cleaning a window at a gas station. Main Street Fuel 'N' More, the sign across the building read. The woman was wearing what appeared to be an orange jumpsuit. The top half was crumpled around her hips.

Her thoughts jumped to Gin and heat stirred between her thighs. Gin was deeply embedded in her thoughts. She'd never met a person who disliked her so much. Hell, she'd never met a person who didn't like her at all. Not even women she'd fucked and sent on their way disliked her. She went to great measures to settle the no-hard-feelings emotion long before it could begin. Nor was she ashamed for being so blunt.

Not once had she been despised. It was unnerving.

Curiosity and a need to see the woman's face got the best of her, and she pulled into the parking lot, then heard a sound she hadn't heard since she was a kid. The distinct double ring of a bell announcing a customer had arrived.

She smiled with the memory of riding in her grandfather's truck, pulling in the gas station, or as he preferred to call it, a filling station, and hearing that exact sound. It was soothing somehow, taking her back in time where she felt protected, where she didn't have to be the protector.

A full-service sign hung over each pump as Carmen came to a stop.

The woman stepped down off the ladder, dropped a squeegee in a bucket of water at her feet, then turned toward Carmen.

Gin. Even the thought of her name sent a chill down her spine. Damn, she looked just as sexy right now, with all those waves spilling out from under that backward ball cap as she had removing that exact attire, weeks ago. Carmen regretted to admit that she'd finished that kiss in her mind over and over and over.

With a start, Gin turned to find a sleek royal blue '68 Camaro pulled against the pump, with Carmen at the wheel, wearing dark sunglasses, hair windblown. Fuck. Did she have to look so delicious? Just when she thought those scalding thoughts were going to fade, here was the woman who had stirred them to begin with, dredging them all back to the surface. Great.

Gin slowly approached the side of the car and dragged a single finger along the metallic mirror finish paint job. No doubt Carmen had fucked a number of women with the seat laid back.

Carmen tilted her head toward the open window, and Gin's stomach knotted. She hadn't expected to see her again. Hadn't wanted to ever see her again. The thoughts alone kept her too close.

But damn if she couldn't stop the rush of heat at the sight of her. Patrick had a point. She was clearly sexually deprived.

Gin took in a deep breath, a little aggravated that Matt wasn't running for the customer, which gave her no other option but to assist this hottie.

She approached the window, her heart skipping a beat.

Carmen glanced down Gin's chest, down the flat of her stomach, and then halted at the bunched material around those lean hips like a lover's hold. Oh, what she could do with those legs.

"Nice chick magnet," Gin said, sarcasm dripping off every syllable.

"Thanks. It helps on occasion." Carmen admired the curve of Gin's breast, how perfect they were. She would have dark nipples to match her sun kissed skin tone, and they would harden against her tongue into delicious pebbles.

"I'm sure it does." Gin propped a hand against the door. "Did you come here to apologize for ruining my date?"

"That date was ruined long before I showed up to save you."

Gin had pert lips. They were kissable. Carmen knew. She'd kissed them. She wanted to kiss them again.

"You think I needed saving? Is that your egotistical brain leading your dick again?"

"Well, I didn't see the other half of your posse, Patrick, anywhere since I knew for a fact that your bestie was out with Phil. But I did see a bored female. Thought I'd lend a helping hand. It's what I do."

"Such a gentleman. You think you need to be a hero both on and off your shift?"

"That depends. Was I your hero?" Carmen offered her best sexy smile.

"You can only be a hero when there's a damsel in distress, begging for help." She held Carmen tight in her sights. "I'm no damsel, never in distress, and I'll never, ever beg."

Carmen couldn't help but shift against the seat to disguise the discomfort from the warmth gathering like a tornadic cloud between her thighs. What she wouldn't give to hear Gin beg. Just once would do. Maybe then she'd have these fantasies out of her mind once and for all. God knew they were causing discomfort.

"I guess that means I won't be getting a thank you?"

Gin tapped a finger against the door. "Exactly. Now, did you need something else? If not, I must get back to work."

Carmen deliberately looked around the empty parking lot. "As a matter of fact, I do need something else, but I'm afraid we'd both get arrested for indecent exposure. Could tarnish my impeccable criminal record. Couldn't have that, now could we?" Carmen silently begged for that exact scenario. Fucking Gin on the hood of this car would be worth being dragged off in cuffs. The energy between them was electric. No denying it.

Gin leaned down in the window, close to those inviting lips, and inhaled the fresh scent of shampoo and soap. Why did she have to smell so delicious and clean? Why did she have to look so sexy behind the shine of this sleek ride? Why did she have to keep watching Gin like she was a meal?

Because that's how the players played the game. They were naturals at luring women in. Absolute naturals.

"In case I wasn't clear before, I don't date firemen, or any other female who uses her uniform to collect midnight fucks. So don't think the hints and blatant invitations have gone unnoticed. I've noticed. You're just not my type. Got it?"

Carmen's gaze dipped to her lips and Gin swallowed. She was so handsome, so determined, and Gin was tempted to crawl through the window to taste another kiss, to straddle her until an orgasm ripped through her body. As horny as she was, she'd only need a few seconds of Carmen's managed time.

But those eyes, even behind the tint of her sunglasses, said so much. Made so many promises. The same promises made and delivered to hundreds, no doubt.

"Got it. But, so you know, midnight is not the only hour on the clock. Nor should you make empty assumptions about a person you know nothing about." Carmen leaned closer to the opening. "But to save argument, to make you feel better about the time of day, I can simply collect yours before the stroke of midnight."

Gin chuckled. "The gentleman shows herself again. Aren't you accommodating?"

Carmen winked. "I try."

"Sweet. But not a fat fucking chance in hell, stud." Gin straightened, pulling away from that undisguised baited line. Mainly because the temptation was too strong that close. She wasn't in a safe place near this woman. "Have a safe day, Carmen." Gin walked away before she was seduced into doing something totally out of character.

Oh, how she wanted to. Right there in the car. On the car. Damn, it was unnerving and downright uncharacteristic how bad she wanted to fuck that woman.

CHAPTER SIX

The night sky was thick with black smoke as Carmen poked at hot spots in the debris on the ground in front of the bookstore. The place had been abandoned for many years and periodically became a hangout for the party animals or homeless. She'd expected a fire long before now. It had been only a matter of time before something like this happened. Luckily, only the middle section had been burned. It wouldn't have hurt her feelings if the whole thing had gone up in smoke. Another month from now, they'd likely be back.

Although, this time felt different. Too many odd fires lately. In unlikely places. Sure, they'd been here more than once, but nothing like this. Nothing so aggressive. And usually, it was the bushes around the place, not inside. Even the homeless had respect for the roof over their head. Her gut said it was more than a group of reckless punks. If she was correct, these sporadic fires were only the beginning. This worrying conclusion nagged at her, and she defied the need to sneak back inside to nose around the area where the fire had originated. Was she being paranoid? Yes. Probably.

She considered whether to share her thoughts, her sudden intrigue with the whole inspection process, with Phil. He would listen and nod while his brow creased in deep concentration, but in all likelihood, he'd leave her hanging for an answer, unwilling to confirm if he thought she was full of shit or if she'd hit the nail on the head.

For some reason, she hesitated to voice her unease. She didn't feel like she would have his full attention. Steph had that now. This budding romance had him by the nuts, and she didn't have the heart to take that smile off his face. Besides, arson investigating, if only through conversation, was out of her league. That was up to the big dogs, and so far, they hadn't been overly concerned. Why they weren't, she didn't know. Her radar was sounding off and theirs should be as well.

A crowd had gathered on the sidewalk beyond the police tape. Beneath the streetlights, Carmen could see them eagerly watching the scene. It was the nature of every human to be nosy. She couldn't stop herself from inspecting each face. She wasn't sure who or what she was looking for. Shit. Yes, she did. She wanted Gin to be among them. Admiring her heroism. Watching her. Wanting her.

She was positive this obsession had stemmed from having her ego bruised not once but twice. How could a person hate another simply for wearing a uniform? Had someone broken her heart? Her spirit? Her soul? It would explain how she was still carrying around all that hostility.

"You ready for the cookout tomorrow night?" Phil yelled from several feet away.

Carmen shrugged. Normally, she was excited about the quarterly bash. It was a special occasion that all available firemen, their families, and friends came together to celebrate life. Over the years, she'd come to understand just how important those times were because the years, months, and days were numbered for them all. Especially hers. She was cursed to be remembered at one of those cookouts, where all the firemen stood together in a circle, beers to the sky, and saluted those who had already crossed over the rainbow bridge.

The more cookouts she attended, the more the celebration reminded her how much closer she was getting to that moment.

"Sure," she lied. "Your new squeeze coming?" The real question was, was the new squeeze bringing her sexy, sharp-tongued amigo?

"Can you believe it? Phil, never-going-to-snag-a-girl-in-his-whole-life, Phil," he bragged, that glimmer of puppy love in his voice.

"Simmer down, Cupid. Let the engine heat up first."

Phil poked at a piece of wood. "You know that clichéd phrase, you'll know it when it happens? I think I know it, feel it, as sappy as that sounds."

Carmen didn't know whether to warn him, to advise him to pump the brakes, but of all the years she'd known him, she'd never seen him quite like this. He couldn't stop smiling when he was talking about her. Like right now, in full uniform, hot, sweaty, tired from hours of fighting a blaze, that smile was dominant.

Her jealousy would be crystal clear if she told him exactly what she thought. That he was going entirely too fast. That he needed to ease off the pedal. Get to know her better. Have his first argument.

That jealousy would show because deep down, she admired those things. Maybe she missed those things. The things she never had. Would never have. But she wanted something. Wasn't this jealousy that was slowly surfacing proof of that point?

She wanted to miss someone. Wanted them to miss her. To get wet from just a memory of them. Makeup sex after an argument. God only knew what that kind of sex would be like with Gin. Feisty, mouthy Gin. What Carmen wouldn't give to tame that tongue.

But this job, the uniform she was born to wear, ensured she would never, could never, have those things. She couldn't be like her brothers, her sisters. She didn't have the heart to share that curse with someone she loved. With someone who had given their heart to her.

So she simply didn't love. No hearts were broken that way. No lives were shattered. No beers to clink at a damn cookout.

"Normally, I'd tell you to back off." Carmen kicked over another smoldering board. "But I don't even own a goldfish so giving you advice on love seems ridiculous."

Phil glanced over at her. "So if I told you I was going to ask her to move in with me, you wouldn't tell me I had lost my fucking mind?"

Carmen studied his expression to see if she found a sign of teasing among that grin. She didn't. Dammit.

"I'd say exactly that—you have lost your fucking mind."

He laughed. "Thank God. You had me scared there for a minute."

"You scared? I just had a flash-forward of you crying at the altar as your bride walked down the aisle."

"Pfft. As if." Phil flipped over a piece of aluminum. "Okay, I might a little."

Carmen chuckled. "You mean a whole lot. You cry when the—"

"Shush your mouth! I do not!" Phil blurted.

"—Browns never, ever, make it to the playoffs," Carmen finished.

"Such a hater, you are."

"So, is Steph bringing her hero-hating serial dater to the cookout?" Carmen regretted the question as soon as she heard the last of it roll off her tongue. She never asked about women. Never. Under any circumstances. Because she didn't think about them once she'd parted from them, that's why. And if anyone knew that fact, it was Phil. He was the closest thing she had to a best friend. He was more than that. He was family. Her brother.

A long pause followed, and Carmen refused to make eye contact. He would be staring at her, brow furrowed, maybe an all-out wide-eyed expression of shock, unsure if she'd lost her mind.

Maybe she had lost it. Maybe she was having an out-of-body experience. God knew she was having an out-of-character moment. The images running through her mind were naughty and hadn't stopped from the second Gin walked away from her car in blatant dismissal. No matter how hard she tried, she couldn't pry the thoughts from her conscious of what one night of sex could do to help her permanently wet situation. All these thoughts, so many of them.

Why? That was the only question that seemed to matter anymore. Simply why.

Phil cackled. "You're afraid of her, aren't you?"

"Screw you."

Phil continued laughing while Carmen resisted the truth. Afraid, yes. Of her, no. Of the fact that Gin was still in her mind, in her wishes, yes. That she wanted a woman who would never want her in return. That she craved a woman who couldn't stand the sight of her.

What the hell was wrong with her? Was it the resistance? The refusal to like her? She wasn't a spoiled brat. She'd been told no several times in her life.

This was deep. It was disturbing her psyche.

❖

Gin's fingers hovered over the keyboard. The words were on the tip of her tongue, on the edge of her lips, yet all she could hear was Patricia's future email chastising her blatant hatred for animal lovers that included an f-bomb, or three.

Lori bored me to tears. I considered masturbating beneath the table while she flipped through her picture gallery of dogs. Yes. I could have come over my fingers while images of rescued Yorkies passed my view.

Actually, that was before another loser, another trained star of the community, attempted to ruin my night. Lucky for me, buff biceps can't knock me off my stance. No matter the career, no matter the bank account, losers will always be crystal clear. But damn, did she look edible. She made me want to crawl across the tabletop, to hell with hiding my masturbation skills in private, spread my legs in blatant invitation, and then shove her face to my crotch and grind against her until...

Gin growled and tapped the backspace button until the page was blank. Wouldn't those paragraphs get Patricia riled up?

Seriously, what had possessed her to agree to this nonsense? This was insane. The dates were useless. The articles were a waste of time. Who the hell was reading them anyway? So far, the only comments to the page were from other serial daters, who already shared her belief, who appeared to be more feminist than Gin cared to be.

She believed in gentlemen. Believed in having her door opened. Her chair pushed under. She wasn't opposed to any of those respectful traits. But she was definitely against someone faking their way through it, just to get her in their bed.

Why was it so hard to find decent people? Why was she cursed to see through their charade, to their true colors, to see all of their closeted skeletons?

With a huff, Gin slammed the laptop shut and leaned back in the chair to stare out the gas station windows. Matt had already gone home for the day. Not a single customer had pulled into the parking lot in three hours. Silence. That's all she'd heard. Fucking silence.

Under the glass, all the way to the right of the desk, two business cards stared back at her. The antique collector was on the very end. Bob Thornton. He'd shown up out of the blue on a bleak and dreary day. The sky had fit her mood. Gray and threatening.

She'd actually been contemplating pulling a chair to the edge of the road, unzipping her coverall to her waist, and flashing cars in hopes that someone would slam the brakes and slide into her parking lot. How else was she going to rope them in on their mad dash to get to the city?

Thankfully, her ridiculous idea had been ended by his arrival. He'd stepped inside the office wearing dark blue jeans with a perfect crease down the legs, a pale pink Oxford, and a brown leather belt. Clean-cut and put together. Silver hair neatly trimmed and a smile that warmed Gin and made her want to ask for forgiveness for her previous naughty intentions.

For the next hour, Gin listened to Bob retell stories about her grandfather, their high school days, how so many guys had fought for her grandmother's attention yet all had failed.

How her grandmother had had eyes for her granddaddy and him alone, that no one could pull her attention away no matter what idiotic stunts they had pulled. Then he'd grinned like he was remembering one of those times.

Gin could envision her nana snubbing her nose and paying none of those puberty driven jocks attention. She'd been good at that. Snubbing people. The woman could hold a grudge like a life preserver. Not because she needed to, but because she didn't play games. If she had a reason not to like you, she didn't like you forever. She didn't offer second chances. Claimed someone who cared wouldn't have screwed up the first chance. Gin was living proof that she had a valid point.

"Stay away from gossipers. If they will gossip with you, they will gossip about you. As my mama said, a dog that brings a bone will carry a bone."

Gin could still hear that lesson. As well as another. *"Love with everything you have. All the way down to your soul, love hard and reckless. Love like you have nothing to lose. And if they screw you over, never throw a tantrum. Smile like you know a dirty secret, like your heart isn't affected, and walk away. Then you live, baby. Live hard. Let karma take care of the rest. She always does. And if you're lucky, she'll let you watch."*

Gin had loved as deep as she could. She'd given it everything. It had cost her a high price. Her soul. As for karma, she wouldn't know. She'd never looked back. But what she wouldn't give to have witnessed that coffee order being delivered to the patrol car, the look of pure panic and shock on Teresa's face, both of them scrambling to cover their naked betraying bodies. A cop, busted fucking a civilian in the back seat of her cruiser. Was that karma enough? Not by a long shot. But it gave her heart a smile to think of their indecent predicament anyway.

Before Bob left that day, he'd given her his business card. "It would be my greatest honor if you would call me if you ever decide to sell the Porsche."

Gin had been startled by the sudden change of conversation. The car had been in the garage so long, she wasn't sure anyone remembered it existed. "I wouldn't hold my breath for that phone call, Mr. Thornton."

He'd gave a firm nod. "I expected as much, nor could I blame you. The car is amazing. But if you change your mind, in working condition, she is worth a quarter of a million. I'll pay every dime."

Gin pushed her feet against the floor and sent the chair into a spin, hoping to whirl some proper words into her brain so she could finish this latest article. And to wipe away the dollar figure from her mind. As well as Carmen's sarcastic, fuck me tone as she walked away from the restaurant.

A quarter of a million dollars would solve all her problems. It would pull the station out of the predicament this new generation had created. She could make improvements. Add that addition on that her grandfather always talked about to include a sandwich and ice cream shop. He was positive it would bring in more customers.

Gin wasn't so sure. She wasn't sure anything would drag the customers away from uptown where the dazzle of the name tag meant more than the quality. Where the car shops herded people into a bay like cattle with their many discount prices.

What happened to people sitting around while their cars were getting a tune-up? To everyone addressing friends by name. Everything had changed. Was still changing.

Truth was, she wasn't sure she even wanted to compete anymore.

Chapter Seven

The sun was just sinking past the tree line when Gin and Steph walked down the driveway of Daniel's home. He was the host for the firemen's cookout tonight. How Steph had finally talked her into coming was beyond her. She didn't want to be here. Didn't want to see Carmen again. Although Carmen had been so webbed into her mind, she might as well be right in front of her, which would be an even bigger mistake. Those images of her up close and personal could have a dangerous outcome. In her thoughts, she'd fucked Carmen repeatedly.

Steph had been giddy the entire ride over, chatting nonstop about Phil, how he was perfect, and funny, and got her.

It appeared she had it bad for the fireman.

Gin wanted that. Again. She'd had that with Teresa. Had that giddiness. The goofy grin that seemed to be a permanent fixture on her lips. The heated memories that seemed to crawl out of her conscious when they were apart. She'd had that. All of it. Then the piece of shit wearing hero's clothing yanked it away.

One day, she was going to find it again. Probably not here. Probably not today. But one day, she'd have that irrational flutter in her gut once again.

However, tonight, her best friend was experiencing all of those emotions and Gin didn't want to be a third wheel in their unfolding romance. She hoped there would be some single women around, even one would do, as long as she wasn't a fireman, and for sure her name couldn't be Carmen. She didn't trust herself around that one.

"We'll scope you out a single non-fireman hottie, and you can pretend it's a date and use it for your next article," Steph said as they stepped onto the porch.

She could do that. She would do that. She had to do that to keep those checks coming in. The bills weren't going to stop piling up so until she got the car fixed, she didn't have a choice.

They were greeted by Daniel's wife, Beth, a petite little brunette with happy brown eyes and welcoming smile. She excitedly chatted as she led them through the house to the back deck where they found Phil among a group of firemen.

His smile radiated as he set eyes on Steph. He jogged over to her and gave her a kiss far too affectionate for these surroundings.

"It's about time you got here. I was worried you'd changed your mind." He pulled Steph into the crook of his arm and looked at Gin. "Thanks for getting my girl here safely."

Gin gave him a nod.

Time seemed to fly as she listened to the group of firemen talk about recent fires, training, how Carmen had robotically saved a toddler from a basement fire.

"What did you expect from our Maverick? Crazy ass thinks that fire is her friend," Phil said.

The mention of her name made Gin warm. She envisioned her in full uniform, rushing into a fire like a warrior. It was disturbingly hot. It shouldn't be.

A woman stepped in front of Gin and held out a beer. "I noticed you didn't have anything to drink. I'm Alexa."

Gin took the bottle and looked down the length of her. Tall, tanned, not wearing a firehouse T-shirt. This could be promising. "Thank you."

Phil gave the woman a warning smirk. "Behave yourself."

Alexa waved him off and turned back to Gin. "Will you allow me to rescue you from these boring heroic stories for a tour of the new water gardens Daniel and I just built?"

Gin greedily accepted by pushing off the railing. "I'd love that." She gave Steph a slight shoulder lift as she moved beside Alexa. The next article had begun.

Alexa led the way down the steps and into the yard where an outdoor kitchen dominated at least a fourth of the grounds. A large gazebo complete with a swing and outdoor furniture was placed close to a water pond filled with bright spotted koi. The place was stunning.

The atmosphere was laid-back, people chattering, laughing, men playing horseshoes, others mastering the grill, kids playing Frisbee and tag. Relaxed. Homey.

Gin didn't feel out of place. She was quite comfortable and could see herself exactly like this one day. A family of her own. Swimming pool for the summer. Cookouts. Neighbors included. She could see it all. One day, hopefully sooner rather than later, she was going to have just that. Even if she had to date her way through the entire female population to find the one who made her ache when they were apart.

"Daniel and I just completed the rock water garden." Alexa pointed toward the edge of the property where a fountain cascaded over large boulders into another fish pond.

"Is this your career?" Gin asked, praying it was. She couldn't deal with another hero today. She'd rather go home and stare at the dust collecting on the walls.

"Yes. I own a landscaping company. We mainly focus on the large business properties, but I help Daniel as often as I can. He's a great guy."

Gin was intrigued and surprised that she wanted to know more about this woman. How was someone so cute, so put together, single? That skeleton was in there somewhere. Weren't they always? She just needed to pry a little deeper to get to the dirty stuff.

"Everything is gorgeous." Gin said, unable to resist another full-body inspection. Tight thighs encased in Levi's. T-shirt loose around her waist. Hand tucked into one pocket. "A woman with working hands. It's sexy."

Alexa grinned and gave a shrug. "I like that you find working hands sexy. Mine are always working. Although, I would prefer softer, curvier things." She gave a wink.

A football landed several feet away. Gin turned to see who had thrown it and found Carmen jogging toward it. Her stomach fluttered.

Wearing another firehouse T-shirt, this one dark blue, slicked against her six-pack abs like a second layer of skin, Carmen looked absolutely edible. That hair was tossed, and she looked like she'd been playing football for hours. Sweat glistened around her neck.

She trapped Gin in a hard stare, bent down, grabbed the football in one hand, and gave a stiff nod before she reared back and threw a perfect spiral back across the yard.

"That's Carmen, the closet football lover," Alexa said. "She claims to hate everything about football, but as you see, every kid in the yard grabs her first. Ain't that right, Carmen?"

"So they claim," Carmen said. "What's up, Gin?" She turned away to wait for a kid to throw the ball back to her.

"You two know each other?" Alexa asked, her hand moving possessively to the small of Gin's back.

"Not really. Just enough to know that Gin kicks ass in pool, hates cheaters, and despises women in uniform." She caught the football and threw it back before trapping Gin in a fuck me stare. "Good thing you're not either of those things. Right, Alexa?"

Carmen turned away and caught another throw from across the yard.

Alexa used the distraction to give a gentle push against Gin's back. "Let's head back up. I'm craving Beth's guacamole."

Carmen watched Alexa herd Gin away with a grumble of jealousy in her gut. It didn't surprise her to see Alexa had jumped on fresh meat. That was her style. No matter how many years she had been married to a devoted wife. The exact kind of person Gin was determined to stay far away from.

The night should be very interesting.

She watched as they found a spot on the outdoor couch, as Alexa possessively wrapped her arm around the back of the cushions, Gin looking at her with pure curiosity, with clear interest.

How was that possible? She was entertaining a cheater, the exact type of person she despised, the exact type of person she had already assumed Carmen was. But she wouldn't give Carmen the time of day, and Carmen was anything but a cheater.

It would be comical if it didn't piss her off so bad. And why was she pissed? Because a female didn't want to be her friend? Oh, if only it was that easy. If only it was that simple.

Her ego was bruised. And it was eating her alive.

She stepped away from the kids and marched up the steps. A beer, maybe three, then it was time to blow this party. There was a bar calling her name. Hopefully with a woman to scream it later.

Gin looked up from the couch as Carmen landed on the top step. She gave Gin an awkward smile before she shook her head and disappeared through the back door.

Why did Gin want to follow her? Why did she want to shove Carmen into a closet then push her down to her knees, ride her mouth until an orgasm shattered all thoughts of her?

It was sick, really. But she couldn't stop her libido from having a mind of its own. She wanted to fuck the player. Just once. One time just to get the taste of her, to be tasted. Then, maybe she would have this unwavering need tucked back down deep in her system where the hell it belonged.

Beth stuck her head out the door as Carmen disappeared through it. "Alexa, Tracy is on the house phone for you. Warning—she has *that* tone. You're in trouble," she said and slipped back inside.

Alexa jerked her arm from around Gin like she'd been burned. She shoved off the couch. "Sorry. I'll be right back."

Gin felt the hair on the back of her neck stand up as Alexa ducked inside the house. No, the fuck this bitch hadn't been flirting with her, teasing her, this whole time with a girlfriend tucked in her back pocket. Well, if that wasn't unveiling the skeleton, she didn't know what was.

Again and again, she kept finding these cheating pissants.

Was another article for the column completed that fast? Could it be that easy?

No. Not this time. She was sick to death of women doing this exact thing. Being this crass. Being this ballsy.

Normally, she would write out her frustration into the paragraphs. Not today. Those words deserved to spill right off the tip of her tongue, right here, right fucking now.

Gin pushed off the couch and barged inside, passing a small group of firemen standing over a bowl of chips and dip, Carmen included, and continued through the great room until she found Alexa tucked into a corner, cordless phone cradled against her cheek.

"Sorry, baby. I don't have a clue where I laid my phone. I've looked everywhere. I miss you, too. No, I was helping Daniel with the water garden. No, we're not done yet. Shouldn't be too much longer."

Gin listened to the babbling liar and resisted yanking a fist full of hair in her grasp and then slamming Alexa's face into the wall. Women just like her, who thought they could do whatever the fuck they wanted in their relationships, got her last nerve. She was sick of it. Sick. To. Death.

She was fuming. Far angrier than she should be. Why? Why did women have to cheat? Why did anyone have to cheat? And why did it make her fighting mad? Because she'd been the woman on the other end of that phone, that's why. She'd been the trusting girlfriend waiting at home. She'd been the woman dangling on the other side. Because someone just like Alexa had ripped her heart in half. That's why.

"No, he's not having a party. That's just the radio. No, there's no women here. I swear. I love only you, baby. There could be a swimming pool full of naked chicks, and I'd still want only you."

Lying ass two-timing piece of shit.

Gin reeled in her rage and stepped in behind Alexa. She ran one hand seductively up her spine.

Alexa flipped around, hazel eyes wide.

Gin pushed herself against that tight body, lips close and teasing, making sure her voice would be crisp and clear to the woman on the other end.

She trailed a finger along Alexa's lips. "I need you to hurry back to bed, sexy. This pussy is getting cold without that hot mouth of yours."

Alexa threw her hand over the mouthpiece, but it was too late. The woman's voice pierced through the air.

Gin stepped back and admired that horrified expression. "You are pure shit. I hope your wife divorces your sorry, pathetic ass."

She spun around and found the group had moved to the door frame, mouths dropped, eyes wide with amusement and shock.

Carmen wasn't smiling.

Gin shoved through them.

Cheers erupted as she bounded toward the sliding door. She was desperate for air, for wide open spaces.

"Coolest shit ever," one voice yelled.

"Busted!" yelled another. "We should have gotten that on video."

"Looks like Alexa is going to be sleeping in the water garden tonight," said another.

Hot, angry tears stung her eyes as Gin stepped out onto the deck, taking in calming breaths, trying to console the inner beast, eagerly searching the yard for Steph so she could say her good-byes.

What the fuck was wrong with everyone? Why couldn't they just be happy in a committed relationship? Or happy not being in one? Why? Why? Why?

Carmen stepped through the door and held a beer out like a peace offering. "Forgive Alexa. She has a good heart but has a hard time keeping that dick in her pants when it comes to gorgeous women."

Gin held up her hand. "Stop. Just stop." She took the beer and swallowed a cooling sip. Then another. And another.

"Stop what?"

"Don't woo me when you and Alexa share the same goal."

Carmen gave her that crooked smile. "What goal would that be, Miss I Know Everything About You?"

Gin hated that smile. No. She didn't. She wanted to wedge it against her crotch. Sick. She was sick. "Notches. You both are only looking for the notches."

Carmen studied her face for several seconds. "Is that so bad if everyone involved knows the rules of the game? Unlike Alexa."

Gin considered her point. Did anyone truly reveal all the rules of the game? Did people really lay all of their cards on the table? Tell the truth? That it was nothing more than a fuck and come morning light, they both would pretend they hadn't shared a night of intimate sex? Did it really operate that way? Could it operate that way?

Was it possible to play a game where hearts weren't on the line? Yes, actually. Yes, it was. She didn't even like Carmen. There was no heart involved. No heart to get bruised. No heart to get broken. She'd be fucking without a single emotion involved.

"No. As long as everyone plays fair." Gin swung her gaze back toward the doors, praying she wouldn't see Alexa through the glass, but silently praying she did. She still had some bottled up anger that needed to be used wisely. "That's the problem. No one plays fair."

Carmen stepped closer, pulling Gin's attention back to her. "Are you ready to finish your demonstration, Gin? Are you ready to play fair?"

Gin studied her expression. She could see the truth in her eyes. No games. No lies. No expectations. No wondering if there was a skeleton in the closet. No need to search for them. Clean fun. Dirty sex. How could she go wrong?

Carmen took another step, erasing the few inches separating them. "Are you ready to be the notch, Gin?"

Gin's anger subsided with the thought of sex. She no longer had an appetite. Well, not for food. Her appetite now included those eyes, Carmen's daring eyes and bold expression, to be staring up at her from between her thighs.

Just one night. She just needed one night with the hottie to get this infatuation out of her system. Yes. She wanted to be a notch. Maybe she would find the answer with the morning light.

Gin turned up the beer and let many gulps slide down her throat. She set the bottle on the table beside her and turned back to a woman she had fantasized about for weeks. "Let me see your phone."

Carmen didn't hesitate. Gin had expected her to. Only God knew how many women's numbers were tucked into that electronic device. Yet, she'd slipped it from her pocket and held it out like her entire life was an open book.

Gin clicked settings, maps, typed in her address, and hit the enter button. She handed the phone back to Carmen. "Keep in mind, I don't do midnight fucks. The clock is ticking."

She turned and left before Carmen could say anything to change her mind. She didn't want her mind changed. Not tonight.

Tonight, she needed to be Carmen's notch.

CHAPTER EIGHT

Gin stood in her garage and stared down over her grandmother's prized possession. A 1962 Porsche 356c that her grandfather had traded for parts and labor with a customer then poured blood, sweat, and tears into refurbishing for their thirtieth wedding anniversary. Gin was almost positive he could have given her twenty more children, just as many grandchildren, a lifestyle of the rich and famous, and she couldn't have loved any of it as much as she loved that car.

Her grandmother had driven it like a boss, complete with her sunglasses and her favorite sun hat. The radio set to oldies rock. The envy of South Carolina, she'd been.

And here it sat in all its chromed and polished glory, on the chopping block to save Gin's future.

The thought of handing this baby over to Mr. Thornton made her nauseous, as if the car had lost out to her grandfather's gas station. One wasn't more important than the other. But only one would bail her out of this shithole. The station had been their livelihood. It had been their entire world. Not the car. By default, it had to be done. But first, she had to get the damn thing running.

Procrastination was the only thing standing in her way right now. Actually, she was standing in her own way, and she was running out of time. It was breaking her heart.

Neither Patrick nor Steph understood the decision she was faced with. Patrick saw a car. Fabulous, he admitted, but still only a car. Not a quarter of a million dollars worth of fabulous, he insisted. And Steph was the most emotionally unattached human being she'd ever met. Talking to her was like talking to a bobblehead.

Not to mention they were barely around lately to rant to. Steph was busy trying not to U-Haul with Phil, and Patrick had been spending a lot more time at the gay club. Gin was almost positive there was a love interest blooming on the horizon. Her best friends, her posse, the complete circle of the buddy system, was moving on with their lives, leaving Gin behind to figure out how to put all the pieces back together. How to operate without their undivided attention.

How did she get to this crossroad in her life? Failed business owner. No love life. Dating for a paycheck just to keep her head above water. With a car that could save her but for the fact it was refusing to crank. And to add the cherry on the top of this mountain of whipped despair, she was reduced to being a fucking notch on a player's bedpost. Willingly, at that. Eagerly, in fact.

She knew she should regret the invitation, but she didn't. It was an honest invitation. No closeted secrets, invitation. It was more than she could say for half of the women she'd dated in the past year. This was just a fuck. Nothing more. No harm done. No foul. Just two willing, capable adults who were fulfilling a need then parting ways without a broken heart.

Lights turned down her driveway and drifted around the garage. Her stomach knotted so tight she had to draw in a breath to loosen the hold.

She scolded herself for the reaction.

Sex. Just sex. She repeated and encouraged herself until Carmen stepped out of her car.

To add insult to injury, she looked just as delicious as she had less than an hour ago.

What seemed like an eternity passed before Carmen came to a stop beside the car. "So this is our stubborn lady?" She peered inside the car and gave a low whistle. "She's sexy."

Gin had no desire to talk shop. She wanted Carmen naked, pinning her down to any surface, and fucking her. They weren't friends now. They weren't going to be friends with the morning light either.

Without responding, because she was afraid her naughty thoughts would spill out as vulgar words, she walked to the garage door and hit the close button. When she turned around, Carmen was closer, those eyes saying she was ready. Gin only needed to make a move, and the charge would be on.

The garage door closed with a bang, and the sound galvanized Gin into motion. She took two steps and then Carmen was in motion, meeting her in the middle. Gin fisted her fingers into the firehouse logo and jerked Carmen into her.

The kiss was exactly as she remembered. Sinfully hot and heavenly perfect.

She expelled a moan as Carmen palmed her ass and easily lifted Gin's legs up around her hips.

Only when the cold steel pressed into her back, did Gin realize they had moved positions, that she was on her back, on the hood of the Porsche. Her head swam as Carmen arched and bucked into her.

Carmen felt too good. The motion of her body, slamming into Gin, was too right.

She raked her nails up Carmen's back and tugged at her shirt, her insides clenching with every bold buck of those hips.

The fire was consuming. She'd never wanted anything more in her life than she wanted Carmen inside her right now. She wanted to scream her name. Wanted the syllables dragged from her mouth. She wanted heat and slick sex and moans jerked from her soul.

Carmen backed out of the kiss and stood, her lips wet and parted. Her gaze stepped over Gin's face, neck, and then came to a stop at the opening of her button-up blouse.

She slowly reached out and fingered the button between Gin's cleavage, teasing and toying and patiently arousing.

Gin arched toward her, begging to be freed, to be seen, to be tasted. "Do it," she panted.

Carmen leaned down, grabbed the folds, and jerked the blouse open. A smile lifted the corner of her mouth as Gin hissed.

She folded her fingers into the hem of Gin's jeans and jerked her upright. Once again, she lifted Gin around her hips. "Point the way, gorgeous, before we leave dents in this beautiful antique. I won't be sorry about it, but—"

Her mouth was against Gin's before she could answer. Her tongue snaked against Gin's, and she started walking toward the door of the house.

Gin squirmed out of her hold as they stumbled through the kitchen, stalling only long enough for another heated kiss against the refrigerator, her arms pinned against the cold surface, magnets hitting the floor without a care. Once again, Gin pushed out of the embrace and led the way down the hallway where Carmen wrapped around her once again just as they turned into the bedroom.

Carmen spun her around, captured her lips once again, then walked her back until her legs buckled against the bed.

She fell backward, and Carmen followed, her mouth latching onto Gin's neck, gloriously igniting fire along her nerves, her skin, her soul. Smoothly, she kneed Gin's legs apart then pressed into her.

Gin greedily ground against the pressure. It was too much. It wasn't enough. Whatever it was, it was incredible, and she didn't want it to stop.

Freedom from any thoughts. Free from guilt. Free from the morning-after worries. It was amazing how liberating she felt, even if she was doing it with a person who would be doing this exact same thing to another woman in less than twenty-four hours. It didn't matter. None of it mattered.

Right here, right now was all that existed and it felt so fucking amazing. So unbelievably right.

Carmen roughly bucked into her and Gin cried out. She drove again, again, and dear God, again.

Gin thrust up to meet every hitch of those demanding hips, desperately tugged at Carmen's pants, their lips still locked together, their panting and moans an erotic mix of sounds.

Carmen leaned back on her heels, leaving Gin to miss her weight, then ripped the button open on Gin's jeans and jerked them down her legs along with her black silk underwear. She licked her lips, suddenly calm under that approving inspection.

"Fucking do something," Gin hissed. "I'm in pain."

"No worries." That taunting smile creased her lips again. "A hero is here to save your day."

Before Gin could scoff at her choice of words, Carmen pinned her legs apart and captured her clit between her lips.

Gin cried out and arched against her mouth, flaming hot trails of liquid heat gathering between her thighs.

Carmen hummed against her pussy, her tongue flicking, lips nursing, and Gin willed her orgasm into retreat, pleading with her body not to cave in so easily. She probed a finger against Gin's opening, teasing to the first digit, then added another and pushed inside her.

Gin expelled a grateful cry and then, despite her self-control, her orgasm shattered. White flashes pulsed behind her closed lids as she whimpered and bucked. Carmen held her legs apart with an easy, firm grip, continuing that rhythmic flutter against Gin's clit. Her body was consumed in the moment, flying high on an endless trail of clenches.

She slammed her palms against the comforter, searching for refuge, for leverage, arching and falling almost uncontrollably. "Fuck," Gin cried.

The pressure against her legs ceased, and then fingers wove into hers. Gin tightened her grip in them and ground her teeth, riding the waves of release, feeling an overwhelming sense of comfort, protection, and finally, her body relaxed. She went limp against the mattress, her hands still entwined with Carmen's.

Seconds, minutes, passed by before Gin opened her eyes to find those delicious chocolate orbs staring up at her from the alcove of her thighs. Lust, probably cocky arrogance, washed over Carmen's expression and then she climbed up Gin's body.

She pinned Gin's arms above her head. "Now that you're no longer sexually deprived, we can begin again." She captured Gin's lips, this time with a slow, gentle ease, released her hands, and rolled Gin on top of her.

Carmen captured Gin's cheeks and deepened the kiss. Mainly because she was afraid Gin would move, would leave, would tell her their time was up. Never had she worried about those words. Normally, she was the one saying them. Why she feared them now, she didn't know. But she wasn't ready to loosen her hold on Gin.

Nothing, not a single sexual moment with another female, had ever felt so linked, so natural, or so genuine. From the kiss to those erotic cries, to the feel of her right now, pressed against Carmen, she'd never felt so alive.

Gin leaned back on her heels and snagged open the button of Carmen's jeans. Carmen had never seen anything look so stimulating, more beautiful than Gin's expression, sexually drained. She tugged the denim down Carmen's legs followed by her thigh-length underwear. Carmen could almost feel the weight of that casual inspection.

She dragged the T-shirt and sports bra over her head while Gin shucked out of her blouse and bra, then pulled Gin back down on top of her. The heat of their skin felt good, comforting. Soft. Had she noticed this before? This wasn't the first time she'd had a woman naked against her. Had they been this warm, too? As soft? As sexy? Had they fit this well? Would she have noticed in the rushed high of sex?

"I need a breath," Gin panted and meant it.

She'd never had an orgasm so fast. So furious. And Carmen appeared eager to begin again.

Carmen captured the skin of her neck with her teeth and gently bit. Gin expelled a moan. Her insides clenched as electric energy paced down her spine, between her thighs. Carmen pressed a kiss against the sting. "Then breathe, sexy."

The trail of kisses and lingering swirl of Carmen's tongue continued into the hollow of her throat, down her chest, before she captured a nipple between her teeth and tugged.

Gin sucked in a startled breath and bowed. She ground her teeth against the intense fire that seemed to have a direct connection to her clit. Good. Her body felt so good. So alive. "I can't."

Carmen rolled her back over and hovered above her, those dark eyes devouring her. Gin saw triumph in those chocolate orbs. She'd won the prize after all. If only Gin cared. For once, it felt damn good not to care.

With that angled smile, Carmen lowered her head, captured another nipple, then rolled the tip between her teeth once again. "Now?"

Gin fisted her fingers into Carmen's hair and arched upward. "No."

Carmen pushed her hand between them, her fingers easily finding Gin's wet opening, and then gently entered her. "Now?"

Gin hissed and tightened her grip even tighter in that handful of soft hair. "No."

Carmen used her knees to push Gin's legs apart, pulling her fingers out to the tips, slowly pushing back in.

"No way in hell I can...do that again." Gin hissed through clenched teeth.

"Then welcome to hell, my pretty." Carmen drove inside her. "Challenge accepted."

Gin screamed out while Carmen bucked against her, inside her, needing to be deeper. To reach deeper. She wanted to touch the core of her, wanted to hear a growl of pleasure that came from the very center of her.

Carmen had never wanted to please anyone more than she wanted to please Gin again. And again. She wanted Gin to scream and beg. To whimper and plead. To hiss and grind. But more than anything, she wanted to hear her own name slip past those lips. She wanted Gin to remember that name, wanted it to haunt her sleepless nights. She wanted that name to drive Gin out of focus every time it entered her mind.

Again and again, she fucked her. Gin locked around her, legs tight, head thrown back. Nothing had ever looked so satisfying. So fulfilling.

Her own orgasm skated the edge while Gin whimpered, while she clutched and tugged.

The orgasm teetered, threatening. Gin's lips were parted, breaths nothing more than shallow gasps. "Open your eyes."

Gin did, her gaze sexually drugged, her insides so damn tight.

Carmen slowed her thrusts. That expression of pure bliss would forever rest in her mind.

Gin's brow briefly angled. "Don't stop."

Carmen ground her teeth against the pressure. Too close to hold back. She bucked into her and pressed her face into the crook of Gin's shoulder.

As if they had been in this position a thousand times before, Gin wrapped her arms around Carmen's neck, cocooning her head, her fingers instinctively entwining in her hair. Her body arched against Carmen's thrusts, her breathing heavy.

Carmen's orgasm clipped the edge, and she bit down on Gin's shoulder.

Gin arched hard, and then her body froze. "Oh...God." Her insides clenched hard around Carmen's fingers and then she started bucking against her.

Together, they rode the waves of pleasure, their bodies arching and grinding, sweat the only thing to separate the heat of their skin.

CHAPTER NINE

Gin padded naked to the bay window. She sat down, lit a cigarette, pulled her knees to her chest, and looked out over the backdrop of the moonlit yard. The moon was bright in the sky, adding a picturesque highlight to her form.

Carmen watched her for several minutes. She was beautiful with her silhouette reflecting off the glass. There was nothing she'd rather be watching. Nowhere else she'd rather be. The realization was comforting as much as it was confusing. She didn't normally have post-sex emotional attractions to women. She couldn't afford them.

These emotions were alien to her, but they didn't scare her. Somehow, she knew they should.

Carmen got up from the bed and joined her on the opposite side of the window seat. "Smoking's bad for you."

She plucked the cigarette from between Gin's fingers, took a draw, then handed it back. Smoking had never been her thing. She needed to stay fit, to never be winded, but the nightclub had pulled that bad habit out of her on several occasions. Strobe lights, loud music, undulating bodies, and one too many drinks seemed to go hand in hand with smoking.

"I always smoke after sex." Gin finally turned to look at her. "A habit I can't seem to break."

"Always?"

"Always. There are a few other reasons that require me to smoke. Reasons I'll keep to myself." She added a mischievous grin.

"Such a mystery, you are." Carmen settled against the windowsill. "Tell me more about that sexy ride in your garage. What's her story?"

Gin shrugged, took another drag, and focused on the view outside the window. She liked that Carmen referred to her grandmother's beloved ride as a she instead of an it. Others might have found it weird, but there was so much history in that car, it made it a living being. It held too many priceless memories to be anything but alive.

"It was my grandmother's."

Carmen simply nodded, no impatience for Gin to continue. To Gin's surprise, she wanted to continue. She wanted to tell Carmen. About the car. About her failing business. About her failure to keep them both running. How she was disappointed in herself.

Gin took a long drag, focused on the fog settling in across the sky, blanketing the grounds. "My grandfather refurbished it as an anniversary present. She was a total boss while driving Ms. Luna."

"Ms. Luna. Got a sexy vibe to it."

Carmen watched her reflection in the glass. Even the darkness couldn't hide the shadow that crossed Gin's expression. The car was the root. The car was the dagger in this story. Gin was more than disappointed. She thought she was failing. Carmen wanted to remind her that the city had swallowed the customers with Starbucks and strip malls and all the fancy restaurants to accommodate the crowd, that the changing economy that was hurting the small shops on the outskirts of town wasn't her fault. But Gin already knew those facts. Her struggle was because of them.

"Ms. Luna will have a new home as soon she gets fixed. She is the sacrificial pawn in this game."

"Meaning?" Carmen took the cigarette again, eager to continue the conversation, desperate for the night to carry on just a little while longer. She didn't want to go home alone. Her little one-bedroom house seemed unpleasantly empty compared to Gin's comfortable bedroom.

She didn't have a corner chair by the window with an afghan thrown over the back. She had a thin bedspread instead of a thick comforter. She had bare walls compared to the paintings and pictures of family and friends that Gin had.

Plain. She felt plain. There was nothing cozy about her home. Why would there be? It was a bachelor pad. Women came. Then they came again beneath her. Then they knew it was time to leave. Because she'd told them as much.

"The car or the business. It appears I can't have both."

"You're selling the car to save the station?" Carmen wanted to warn her, to remind her that her property, a lone gas station on the outskirts of town could be prime real estate for the automotive industry rumored to be looking in their territory. Joined with the bare land around it, she had no doubt that someone would pay top dollar. Otherwise, selling the car was only buying her time, not solving her long-term problem.

Gin could hear the concern in Carmen's voice. She didn't like it. Didn't like being pitied. Didn't even like Carmen. Carmen stood for everything Gin had fought hard to stay away from since she walked away from a cheating cop.

Yet, right now, she was more content, more satisfied, than she had been in years. She wished she could be ashamed. She wasn't.

This night would end soon. They both would move on with their lives, they would nod or wave when they passed each other, which was more likely to happen than not considering both of their best friends had found love with each other, and one day they would barely remember this night, those erotic cries of passion.

The acknowledgment made her a little sad. Carmen was incredible in bed. Very intuitive. Rough at just the right moment. Easy when necessary. She was a great lover. But Gin wanted loyalty in her life. She needed trust. Demanded it, in fact. She would have neither with a woman like Carmen.

She took the cigarette back from Carmen. "We all make sacrifices in life. Mine pales in comparison to yours."

"Oh, now you think my job is cool?" Carmen said.

"Just because I don't like you doesn't mean I can't admire your heroism." Gin took the last toke and snuffed the butt out in the ashtray. "You do what fifty percent of the population could never do. It takes guts."

"You still don't like me?" Carmen cocked a playful brow.

"Not even a little bit." She gave a half smile. "Doesn't mean we can't pretend for our friends, though."

Carmen crossed her arms over her knees. "So, Gin, tell me. Was it a fireman or a cop who broke your heart?"

Gin studied her expression. There was no judgment in her eyes. She didn't owe Carmen anything. No explanation. Not even an answer. But for some reason, she didn't mind sharing. Maybe she wanted to. "Cop," she whispered.

"Ouch. I'm sorry."

"Don't be. I've come to accept that my judge of character is warped." Gin added a chuckle. "If I can't trust a hero, who the hell can I trust? So I've taken it upon myself not to trust anyone. Especially heroes."

"Come here," Carmen demanded.

Gin wanted to resist. She wanted to tell her to leave, that their fuck with no heartstrings attached, was over.

Something in those two little words made her want to move. Made her want to erase the space between them. Made her want to crawl into Carmen's lap and grind against her.

Instead of resisting, she scooted over and straddled Carmen's lap, lured by those commanding eyes. By the soft and sexy way she'd said those words.

Carmen captured her lips, one hand wrapped around the back of her neck, while the other moved between Gin's legs.

Gin hummed against her mouth, aware that her body was sparking to life all over again.

Carmen pushed inside her and Gin moaned. She withdrew then pushed inside again.

Gin rode her, arching and lifting, her orgasm scrambling to the razor-sharp edge, amazingly, again.

"Trust me when I say I'm going to make you come again," Carmen whispered against her lips then snaked her tongue back inside Gin's mouth, swirling and tasting and possessing.

Gin hummed and arched, rising and falling, until the orgasm ripped through her body. She bowed back, her insides squeezing Carmen's fingers, held securely by the single, strong hand around her neck. Somehow, she knew Carmen wouldn't let her fall.

When her muscles stopped their rhythmic spasms, Gin sagged against her.

Carmen snuggled into the crook of her neck and wrapped Gin in her arms. The embrace was warm and comfortable and so right it was wrong. She didn't like feeling good in Carmen's arms. Didn't like the contentment. Didn't like that even as she mentally argued with herself about how wrong this truly was, she was tightening her hold around Carmen's neck.

Carmen smelled so good. Her embrace protective. No doubt she drove half the female population to drool on themselves. The player who was good at playing the game, because that's what heroes were supposed to do.

But so did Gin. She refused to play Russian roulette. The confirmation of her beliefs was enough to drag her common sense back to the surface.

Gin inhaled Carmen's scent for the last time, then pulled her arms from around her neck. She eased off the lap of a hero who should have never made it to second base, let alone been able to do a home run trot after this night of fucking. Yet, she was here, and Gin couldn't feel guilty.

"Thanks for the non-midnight fuck." Gin turned before she could read anything in those eyes that would make her change her mind, make her crawl back into that lap, back in that bed. "Could you please lock up on your way out?"

Carmen watched her walk calmly across the room and disappear into the bathroom.

Shock resonated as she heard the water turn on.

She'd just been dismissed. She'd been fucked, had done the fucking, and now she was being relieved of her sexual duties. This was normally her line with the women she picked up. Fuck them, then dismiss them. It was always easier that way. No one got hurt. No one held on to hope for a second date.

But the tables had been turned on her. She was on the receiving end of that slap in the face and it stung. Had her honesty with the women she fucked deprived any of them of this feeling when she concluded their night? She prayed it had. She never wanted to hurt anyone. That's why she was so brutally honest with them.

Confused, Carmen pushed off the window seat and started searching for her clothes, long dismissed in the throes of passion.

She donned each piece, her heart a little heavy, her ego more than bruised. With one last glance toward the open bathroom door, hoping Gin would change her mind and invite her in, Carmen finally let herself out the front door.

Chapter Ten

G in wrestled with a bolt on an alternator while Matt watched from across the engine without much interest. She'd caught him several times watching the cars pass along Main Street.

"Am I boring you?" She gave him a smirk while she pushed against the wrench, bracing her knees against the bumper to get more leverage. The bolt broke loose and sent her knuckles slamming against the housing. "Fuck!"

She pulled out from under the hood and stuck the bleeding finger in her mouth.

Every day, the same shit. She had once lived for this station. She'd wake each morning bright-eyed and bushy-tailed, normally beating her grandfather to the dining table for breakfast, especially, and always, getting to the truck long before he even stepped out onto the porch. He had adored her enthusiasm. Wouldn't he be disappointed to see her now?

Now, she barely had enough gumption to unlock the front doors every morning. What was the use? A few straggler customers, mainly travelers who had ventured too far off the freeway, were the only faces she saw. She still had a few repeat customers who came to the shop for small repairs, but even those were getting scarce.

She understood why Matt would rather dig in dirt. Maybe she should join him.

"You okay?" Matt asked, avoiding looking directly at the blood.

He was such a strange kid. Manly, with a feminine side. Not gay, but probably misunderstood by many.

As odd as he was, she was proud to have worked with him all these months, no matter if his lack of passion had gotten on her nerves. He was no mechanic. He was far from his calling. She couldn't wait for him to reach the same conclusion. But she was grateful to have the cheap labor. Not to mention, he'd spruced up the grounds with bright flowers and evergreens, courtesy of his father's nursery. She didn't have the heart to tell him that if the white towel hit the ground, if, when, she was forced to sell this beloved place, his little garden would be plowed over with the bricks.

"Let's take a break." Gin wrapped the rag from her pocket around her finger. "I have some computer work to take care of, and I'm sure you're dying to get back to playing in the dirt." She resisted rolling her eyes.

This kid needed to get the hell out of her shop where he clearly didn't belong. If she fired him, would he realize the place he'd been avoiding was where he belonged all along?

"Yes, ma'am. I'll be in the back if you need me." He darted out of the bay before Gin could tell him she was kidding, something she'd done a few times when he'd gotten too serious over some repair.

She dug a Band-Aid out of the first aid kit then plopped down in her desk chair.

Her latest column stared back at her. Alexa, renamed, Lexie, was the object of her poisonous tongue today. Once again, she'd hit a roadblock with her words. The real words hiding just beneath the surface. Patricia had muzzled her true voice.

As if summoned, her thoughts snapped to Carmen, and her crotch heated. Their night had been incredible. Incredible enough for Gin to still be thinking about it all these weeks later.

No doubt Carmen had already moved on. Several times. The thought made her growl. She'd slept with a cheater. A player. A hero. Whatever had she been thinking? She'd fucked a fireman. Albeit, an honest one who hadn't hesitated to let Gin know exactly where their night would lead. Nowhere. Their time together, all glorious hours of it, would lead to nowhere.

A notification pinged on her computer, and she looked down to find a new message from Match-Us. Pamela. Computer programmer. Enjoyed long hikes, ice cream, and baking. Didn't care much for dogs.

"Yes!" Gin chanted, relieved and optimistic that she wouldn't spend any amount of their date flipping through a gallery of fur babies.

She wasn't a cop. Or a first responder. And thank God, she wasn't even a volunteer fireman.

Gin didn't have a choice but to accept. Of course, her idea of an ideal first date would have never been at a bakery, but hey, everything else had crashed and burned, why not see where frosting tips would lead her? Besides, Pamela had already scored points for simply being a boring nobody. Not to mention, if all else failed, a paycheck and another date pushed her closer to the end of this assignment. Not that she had a backup plan in the works. The paycheck from these articles were at least paying some of the bills.

She sent back a reply that she would love to go on a date, yes, tonight at the bakery uptown was great, then sent Steph a text to see if she was free. Just in case. Of course, with her time being consumed with Phil and their ever blooming romance, Gin didn't expect her to be.

Steph: Phil is dying to tag along. Send me the place and time and we'll be there. Miss you!

Gin: Miss you, too, Cinderella.

Steph: Don't be a hater. *grin*

Gin didn't respond. Yes, she was being a hater. Hated that she was missing her friends. That they were beginning to move apart from her. What would she do with herself when she was all alone? When they were too busy for drinks or movie nights or shopping sprees?

She was going to die alone. Dammit. She was going to become that fucking cat lady.

❖

Carmen was putting away dishes in the mess hall, eager for her shift to end when Phil bounced in.

"Hey. What are you doing tonight?" he said.

"Depends on why you want to know."

"Want to come watch the girls in action? Gin has a date at the bakery uptown, and we need a plus-one. Patrick has to work."

She looked at him over her shoulder, brow raised. "Are you supposed to sound this excited, Martha Stewart?"

He shrugged with no hint of embarrassment. "You haven't read the articles. They're hilarious. These girls are insanely clever when it comes to ditching a bad date. Come on. It'll be fun. What else do you have to do?"

First off, Carmen had no desire to watch Gin on a date, no matter how the date ended. Second, a bakery? What woman took someone to a bakery for their first date? Third, what if the date didn't end badly? What if they hit it off? How would she feel?

She couldn't stop thinking about Gin, their night together, getting the shaft when Gin had gotten all she wanted from her. It was hard to admit, even if only to herself, but she was still a little scorned. Not once in her life had she been dismissed so easily. Without hesitation. As if Gin had practiced that exact line a hundred times.

"Cut the grass with a pair of scissors? Get a root canal? Pluck out my eyebrows? Repair plumbing pipes after forgetting to cut off the water first?"

"You're jealous," Phil said. "Admit it."

"Reverse psychology doesn't work on me." Carmen continued putting plates away so he wouldn't see the truth in her eyes. Yes, dammit. She was probably jealous. The thought of being so close to her, while another woman begged for her attention, left a sour taste in her mouth. "I'm not interested in Gin." Another lie.

"That's what I told Steph when she asked."

Carmen put another plate in the cabinet and tried to erase the curiosity from her mind so it wouldn't be so genuine in her voice. God knew she wanted to hear the answer. "What did Steph ask, exactly?"

"If you had told me about your sex-filled night with Gin. I assured her you didn't kiss and tell." Phil pulled himself onto a stool and settled into the conversation.

"You know me well, my friend." Carmen was more curious what Gin had said. Had she shared the good stuff or had she opted to keep those moments to herself? Or maybe Carmen had misjudged those cries of passion. Maybe their time together had been the worst of Gin's life. She might have been called a loser in and out of bed.

"And what exactly did Gin tell her?" The question was out of her mouth before she could stop it. This time, she didn't care if Phil gave her a confused stare or if the curiosity was laced in the words. She needed that answer to kiss the boo-boo on her ego.

"Just that you guys had a little roll in the sack. Said it was no big deal," Phil said almost with glee.

No big deal? Hour after hour, they'd had that little roll in the sack. Her cries of release had been exotic and unfiltered. And she called that no big deal?

Why did she feel belittled all of a sudden? How did Gin continue to punch her pride?

"True. It was no big deal," Carmen finally added.

"I never doubted otherwise. So you'll come with us?" Phil pleaded.

"Yes. But you'll owe me a big one."

Phil slapped his hand on the counter. "You're awesome! Meet me at the bakery at seven."

Hours later, Carmen pulled into the parking lot of the strip mall, no doubt the reason Gin's station was in trouble, and found Phil and Steph sitting on a bench in front of the bakery. She'd only visited the place once to pick up a cake order for one of the firemen's birthday party. In the back, they had cake decorating classes. You could make an appointment or simply walk in, if she remembered the sign correctly.

She parked the car and joined the lovebirds on the sidewalk, scanning the interior through the glass for long auburn hair. Did Gin know that Carmen was the plus-one tonight? How would she feel about it?

Steph wrapped Carmen in a tight hug. "Thank you so much for coming. Patrick was busy tonight. I think he's got a pretty boy he's been hiding from us."

"Don't thank me yet. Depending on what my role is, I still have time to bail."

"Oh no, you don't. I've been feeling all kinds of guilty for leaving my girl hanging these past few weeks. Thirty minutes, tops, she'll throw the sign, we can have a little fun with her rescue, and you can be back on the road to your original nightly plans."

Carmen wanted to correct her. Truth was, she didn't have anything else to do. No nightly plans. She'd visited the bar three times in the past few weeks and had barely finished a beer before she was ready to leave. She missed her sidekick. Not to mention what, who, she wanted wasn't going to be at the bar. Who she wanted was probably out on another date, hopefully not smoking that after-sex cancer stick. That bothered her the most. God only knew why.

"I told Phil he would owe me one for this. But you can pay up now by answering one question." Why something so unimportant still nagged her, she didn't know. But it did, and she needed to know once and for all.

Steph gave a knowing smile. "You want to know what the signal was at the bar that night?"

Shocked that she was so easy to read, Carmen gave a single nod.

Steph gave Phil an *I told you so* expression before looking down at the sidewalk. "I had a feeling it was bothering you." She glanced around as if she were about to reveal top secrets. "One arm around your neck. Instead of two. That was the signal."

Carmen thought back to that night. To the kiss that had stirred an awakening deep down inside her. An emotion that was still awake all these weeks later, that had only grown, deepened, after their little roll in the sack, as Gin had so delicately put it. Gin's arm around her neck, her fingers woven into her hair. She'd found it seductive. Obviously, it wasn't.

She snickered. "Consider tonight paid in full. So what am I supposed to be doing in this game of charades?"

"That depends." Steph sat on Phil's lap. "How good are your acting skills?"

Fifteen minutes later, Carmen had been given the highest level of signals, sworn to secrecy, and threatened with her life if she admitted any of them to Gin. She tried to repeat them in her head. Twirling hair repeatedly meant someone needed to call her cell phone with an emergency. Unless her hair was up. In that case, the sign would be fidgeting with an earring. If by chance, she wasn't wearing earrings, which wasn't normal on a date, she would scratch her neck. If her hair was down, she would flip it over her shoulder. That meant either of the amigos could rescue her from the date however they wanted. Hence, when Steph pretended to be the jealous ex.

Or did she have everything backward? Shit.

"Don't worry if you forget. Took us years to perfect the signals," Steph said, her arm tucked around Phil's waist. "Keep an eye on me if you think you missed a sign, okay?"

"Sure." Carmen straightened, not sure if she was ready to step inside the store, more unsure if she wanted to see Gin's face again. "Let's get this party started."

"Yay! You go in first. We'll come in a few minutes behind you. Take the table as close to her as you can get. Preferably behind her." Steph gave her a little push, and Carmen stepped through the door.

Chapter Eleven

A cute young high school girl in a black striped smock leaned against the counter and greeted Carmen. "Welcome to Spartan Bakery. What can I get for you tonight?"

"I'm here for the classes." Carmen kept moving, afraid if she stopped, she'd change her mind. "Thank you."

A warning voice screamed in her head. She shouldn't be here. Shouldn't be involved in the buddy system. Shouldn't be involved with Gin. At all. But she liked Gin. That was the problem. She shouldn't like her. Gin couldn't stand Carmen. That bothered her the most. The fact that someone couldn't stand her for reasons all their own.

Mentally arguing with herself, Carmen deliberately put one foot in front of the other until she entered the back room. Eight waist-high tables in two rows of four lined the center of the room.

She spotted Gin on the front row, facing away from the door. Wearing a mosaic print sundress with the back cut out to the curve of her waist, her hair twisted into a loose French braid that cascaded over one sensual shoulder, she was the epitome of class and sex appeal.

But Carmen knew she was anything but those things. She was hellfire and hard. She was soft with a sharp tongue. Yet, in the vortex of non trust, was a trusting soul. A bruised soul. And she didn't like people. Gin never played well with strangers.

Carmen wanted to play again. Just once. And then she wanted to leave Gin right where she'd found her. Pissed at the world, wearing blinders but searching for the light at the end of the tunnel.

Without waiting for instructions, she took the empty table directly behind Gin and her date. To her right was a biracial couple who were already discussing food coloring and icing tips. In front of them was a woman who had her items organized perfectly across the table from large to small. To her left, a very tall man wearing black-rimmed glasses stared straight ahead, intently listening to the instructions already underway.

The remaining tables were empty.

Minutes later, Steph and Phil took the table to the far back left.

Carmen couldn't tear her sights away from the indention of Gin's dress, where it caressed the curve of her hips, dangerously close to the slit of her ass cheeks. Where she wanted to put her hands, her mouth, her breath.

Gin's date stood a good foot above her. Dark hair, broad shoulders, and pale blue eyes that hadn't left Gin from the second Carmen walked into this room.

"The inner tip fits into the bag, like such," the female instructor continued. "And the metal tip pushes onto the outside, like so."

Gin's date attempted to follow directions before dropping the bag, dropping the tip, and cackling at her clumsy fingers. "I swear I've done this before. I'm just so nervous this close to you. You're stunning."

Yes, she was. The words, packed with such meaning and intention, made Carmen's jaw clench. She wanted to say those words to Gin. She wanted to tell her how beautiful she was tonight. How much she wanted to crawl up inside that dress, hike Gin's leg around her shoulders, then make a feast out of her.

"Here. Let me do it." Gin took the bag and tip then proceeded to put them together. "There."

"You look amazing," the date said, her please, I'm begging you, screw me eyes, dripping over Gin.

Gin smiled up at the woman. "Thank you. You look pretty handsome, yourself."

Carmen felt a talon claw at her gut, and she reeled in the need to expel a dramatic grumble, to rush around the table, toss Gin over her shoulder, and march out of this damn bakery.

To stop the uncharacteristic emotion, and because she could almost read the bored expression in Gin's eyes because she could hear the fakeness in her voice, she looked around the man beside her and found Steph staring back at her, a wicked grin on her lips. She shrugged and gave Carmen a thumbs-up.

What the hell did that mean? That the date was going great? That she should keep watch? How the hell did she get here? How had she let Phil talk her into this nonsense?

Bullshit. Phil hadn't talked her into anything. She'd wanted to do this. Wanted another night ripping erotic moans from Gin. From the looks of the date so far, even if Gin was going to fake her way through it, that was a fat chance. That alone made her gut tighten even harder.

"When you're ready, mix the food coloring into your icing until you get the desired shade, spoon it into your bag, and you can begin icing your cakes. Let me know if you need help." She pointed first to Carmen then to Phil's table. "Let me get our newcomers a cake from the fridge. I'll be right back."

Gin turned around at the mention of a newcomer, unaware that anyone else had joined the class since her date found it necessary to tell her umpteen million times that she was either pretty, beautiful, remarkable, or stunning.

Weren't those the things that any female wanted to hear? Isn't that what every female wanted? Attention? To be coddled? Sure it was. But not when it was driven down her throat. Not when it was fake. Gin could tell. She wasn't an idiot. Not to mention, she was kind of a pro at spotting the carbon copy of losers. But she was game to see where this date would lead. Not to mention, it was another date knocked off the contract.

She froze when she found Carmen looking gloriously tasty in a slouchy white button-up shirt with the sleeves rolled up to her elbows, dark blue jeans, and her hair finger-combed. Shit. She looked just as edible out of her firehouse T-shirt as she had in it. Dammit. She looked just as good down to her glorious nakedness.

What the hell was she doing here?

Carmen nodded to the left. Gin followed her direction to find Steph and Phil grinning like fools. No Patrick.

No way in hell Steph had called Carmen in to play the buddy system in his absence. She wouldn't. Wouldn't dare. Yes. By God. She would. She had.

Gin gave Carmen a warning scowl and turned her attention back to her date, her body fully aware how close Carmen was. Heat sparked as she recalled their night together, the way Carmen had brought her body to life. The way she wanted her to do it again.

No, the fuck she didn't. No. No. No. Even as she mentally argued with herself, her body mocked her silly lies with a tightening between her thighs. Carmen had worked a little magic there. Magic she couldn't shake.

The instructor scurried back out with two cakes. She gave one to Steph and Phil without so much as a glance, then paused at Carmen's table. She slowly placed the cake on top, watching Carmen intently. "Couldn't help but notice you were all alone. Will someone else be joining you?"

Carmen caught Gin looking over her shoulder and liked the spark of jealousy in her eyes. "No, ma'am. I'll be flying solo tonight."

The woman fingered her bottom lip. "Fabulous. You'll let me know if you need my help, won't you? It would be my pleasure. My name is Marla, by the way."

Carmen gave Marla what she hoped was her sexiest smile. "I may take you up on that offer."

Marla seemed pleased with Carmen's answer. She gave a flirtatious smile then moved between the tables to check on everyone's progress.

Without really paying attention to what she was doing, Carmen added several different drops from the food coloring to the mixing bowl of already prepared white frosting, then stirred. Her attention continued to move to Gin, waiting for the sign. If she could remember what any of the signs were, that is. Something about her hair. Which looked better down, fisted in her hand. Playing with her earrings? She wasn't wearing any. Twirling? Yes. That was part of it. But how was she going to twirl hair that was twisted into a braid? Wait, Steph had told her that part, too. Her neck. Something about her neck, which looked inviting at the moment.

But that dress. That dress was meant for removing. It was meant to hit a floor, to lie in a heap while sounds of sex moaned around it.

Carmen groaned out loud.

She added several more drops of every color on the table, truly not caring what shade she created.

"Nice job with the colors." Marla moved up beside Carmen. She slid her hand across the table and lightly fingered Carmen's arm. "I like a woman who isn't afraid to be bold."

When Carmen glanced up, Gin was glaring in their direction. Her expression matched Carmen's inner beast. Jealous. Gin was jealous. The same emotion that rested in Carmen's gut every time her date splayed a hand down Gin's back, entirely too close to the curve of her ass.

With those smoldering eyes bearing down on her, Carmen wanted to twirl her own damn hair. She wanted to flip it, pull it, whatever it took to end this useless date.

She wanted that gorgeous body beneath her and those eyes staring up at her as an orgasm ripped through her body. Goddamn, she wanted that so bad it made her body hum.

To hell with the buddy system. She had her own scheme to end this waste of their time. Time that could be better spent naked, with that dress hiked up to Gin's throat, with Carmen nursing her clit. Yes. She wanted that time. Again.

"I'm bolder than you can possibly imagine," Carmen said, her eyes still locked on Gin.

That stare told her that before the stroke of midnight, Gin was going to come over her fingers, over her mouth, again, and again, and again.

"But not as bold as this beauty is." Carmen pointed the stirring knife toward Gin. Gin's eyes widened as the date turned around to face the conversation. Carmen charged on, too far gone to stop now. "Loud print dress, no bra, nipples erect and proud, and that slit cut down to the curve of such a sweet ass, teasing every eye in the room." She started stirring the frosting again. "A dress like that begs for attention. Although I bet she doesn't beg." Carmen looked back up and locked her sights on Gin. "Do you, beautiful? Do you beg?"

Gin opened her mouth to respond then quickly clamped it shut. She heaved in a breath as if it took genuine effort.

"That was completely disrespectful. You need to apologize now." The date turned to face Carmen, planting her hips shoulder width apart in a dominating posture, arms down by her side.

Carmen casually licked the icing from the knife, fully aware that Gin's date had her by a few good inches, several pounds, a fact that common sense couldn't be bothered with right now. "That so?"

"Yes. You need to tell this sweet, and yes, beautiful woman, you're sorry. Right now," the date demanded.

Carmen turned the knife around and licked the opposite side with just as much casual ease. She watched Gin watch her. "Did my blatant approval offend you, sexy?"

Gin nervously rubbed one hand up her arm which pushed her cleavage together, pushing those hard nipples tighter against the fabric. She narrowed her eyes at Carmen. "Would a girl wearing a dress cut down to her ass get offended easily?"

Carmen pushed the knife between her lips and sucked off the last of the icing. "Quite the opposite. You look like someone who was turned on by my detailed observation. Are you? Are you turned on…Gin?"

The date whipped around to face Gin. "Do you know this woman?"

Steph gasped. Phil chuckled.

Gin cocked her head to the side, her lips pressed tightly together, eyes dancing with humor, maybe even a little anger. The lust laced in her expression was all that truly mattered.

Carmen was not ashamed. This date was coming to an end fast.

No, it was all but over. Soon, Gin was going to be beneath her. Those nipples were going to be between her teeth. That ass was going to be in the palm of her hands while she drove inside her before Gin screamed out with her orgasm.

The image danced clearly in her mind. Her insides throbbed.

Tires loudly squealed outside the bakery followed by the unmistakable sound of an impact. The echo of shattering glass pierced the room.

Carmen dropped the knife and shoved away from the table. She bolted through the door before Gin could even register the movement.

"Call nine-one-one!" Phil yelled and charged from the room as well.

Chapter Twelve

The instructor darted for a cell phone on her desk against the back wall. "Oh, Lord. Oh, Lord. Oh, Lord," she chanted as she punched buttons and then jogged for the front door.

"Come on, Gin! Let's go!" Steph yelled and darted from the room, worry and excitement etched on her expression.

"You know her, too?" her date asked, blue eyes narrowed before lowering to Gin's cleavage. "What the hell is going on here? What kind of game are you playing?"

Gin felt one second of guilt. Maybe half of a second. "I'm sorry. I have to go." She bolted around her and raced after Steph.

The sidewalk outside the bakery was lined with onlookers, all facing the parking lot.

Gin fell in behind Steph as she pushed through the crowd until they got to an opening. Several people held up their phones as they captured the chaos. Nothing was private in this new era of technology.

Steph grabbed her arm and pulled her further, past the line of gawkers and between parked cars, until they came to a clearer vantage point of the accident.

Gin's breath caught as she took in the sight of a minivan nose first in a power pole. The windshield was shattered. Smoke billowed up from under the hood and steam hissed. Water ran in a stream across the asphalt.

Two other cars were in the road. One was facing the wrong way with the driver's side T-boned. Gin couldn't tell what kind of car it was, only that it was silver. A third car sat several yards behind the second, the front end crushed. That one was a four-door Honda. Smoke plumed from beneath the hood.

Carmen moved robotically around the van, shifting from window to window, talking to the passengers inside, while Phil ran for the car facing the wrong way, which seemed to have the most damage. Carmen ordered everyone inside the van not to move, that help was on the way.

"Check the kids!" the male driver begged, blood running down his forehead.

With quick movements, Carmen checked the gash in his head and must have been satisfied that he would be okay. She opened the sliding door and climbed inside to examine the two kids in the back, a boy about eight and a girl about ten who seemed frazzled and excited but not injured.

"Oh, wow. Wasn't expecting that." Phil took a few steps back from the T-boned car, his hands up defensively, and yelled out, "Can someone get me a blanket? Or two?" He turned his back to the open window and looked toward the third car.

"Oh no. Do you think they're dead?" Steph echoed Gin's thoughts as her attention was dragged back to Carmen.

The mom in the passenger seat of the van was sobbing and desperately trying to look over her shoulder. "Are they okay? Are my babies all right?"

"Yes, ma'am. They're doing great," Carmen assured her as she moved her attention back to the front seat. "Kids love this stuff. You have made their day."

Mom relaxed. "Thank you, God." She shoved her hands against the dash. "Can you help me? I can't move my leg."

Carmen opened the opposite sliding door and jumped out. She opened the passenger door to get a better look. Her hands moved under and over the woman's leg. "It's not broken. Just pinned." She tested the cracked plastic, which seemed very loose despite the way it was pressed into the cabin, then looked up over the hood. "Can someone find me something to pry with?"

Several men scattered toward the parking lot as Carmen moved back to the woman.

"Relax, ma'am. I promise we will have you free in no time." She motioned for the kids who had crept into the middle seats. "Your mom's going to be just fine. Come give her some loving for a few minutes, then you can help me rescue her. Okay?"

The kids brightened and nodded adamantly.

"Here! Will this help?" A man ran toward the van with a granddaddy pry bar.

"Perfect." Carmen took the tool. "Can you please get me a head count and progress on that car?" She nodded toward the third car.

The man scurried away.

"Okay, guys. You ready to be heroes?" Carmen asked the kids.

"Yes!" they screamed in unison.

"Great. Little man." Carmen nodded toward the boy. "I need you to show me your Superman strength and hold Mom's arm against the console. Not too hard. We just don't want her to go flying out of the van. Can you do it?"

"Yes." His expression turned serious, his lips set in a determined line.

Mom, understanding what Carmen was up to, placed her arm between the seats on the center console. She moved her other hand over her head, and the daughter grabbed it.

Carmen moved her attention to the little girl. "You, sweetheart, need to hold Mom's hand until it's over so she doesn't get scared. Can you do that for her?"

The little girl nodded and gripped her mom's hand in both of hers.

"Are you both ready?" Carmen held up the pry bar for their inspection.

"Ready!" they both cheered.

Carmen moved the tool beside the woman's leg while Dad reached out and took Mom's hand.

Gin was touched by the moment. Carmen being the cool fireman that the kids would never forget. Nor would they forget how they had all come together to save their mom, even if the kids never knew she wasn't in imminent danger. They would talk about it every chance they got.

Carmen gave a fake grunt as she pushed against the broken dash. The plastic gave easily, more than enough room for Mom to move her leg, but instead, she continued to play along.

"It's okay, Mom. We're gonna save you," the little boy said.

Carmen gave another fake grunt, and the plastic moved back again.

"Squeeze my hand if it hurts too bad, Mom," the little girl said.

Carmen gave another groan, pushed against the dash, and suddenly, the woman was free.

It was the cutest thing Gin had ever witnessed, and she wished she could freeze everyone around her so she could press her body against Carmen. She wanted her lips locked with hers, wanted her tongue in her mouth, wanted Carmen's heated breath feathering against her inflamed crotch.

She'd never wanted anyone so bad. So bad it made her ache. It was a sick reaction considering the circumstances, but she was without willpower to struggle out of the need.

"There's a woman in here," the man screamed out.

"Carmen, we have a neck injury but stable. And, um, well, you'll see," Phil yelled from the car facing the wrong way as a woman ran forward with a blanket and thrust it out for Phil.

He handed it through the open window and Gin saw a hand reach out to take it. Not dead. That was good.

Carmen gave the kids a high five, then told them they had been so brave and when Mom got all better, to come by the firehouse so she could thank them properly for their assistance. Their smiles were huge as she turned toward the third car.

"Fire!" a woman screamed from the crowd. "There's fire under the car!"

"Everybody, get back!" Carmen ordered as she ran for the car.

The crowd pushed backward, and gasps washed over them in waves.

As if triggered by the sound alone, Phil charged for the car.

Carmen's arms pumped, her back muscles bunched, as she sprinted down the street. It was fucking hot, and Gin had to swallow.

Phil beat Carmen to the driver's door and jerked on the door handle. He jerked again, harder, as if he could pry it off the hinges, his instinctive determination was the part of him, the hero part of him, that needed to save a life.

More cars were stopped in the street, their occupants all gathered nearby to watch the scene unfold.

Gin stepped closer, lured by the drama. Lured by Carmen in action, the way she had dived into the chaos like she was born specifically for this job.

Carmen never stalled. Never hesitated at the sight of those orange flames licking the ground. Her arms kept pumping until she reached the car.

She slid across the crushed hood like Luke Duke, as if she'd perfected, created, that very move, and landed on her feet on the opposite side of the car. She checked the door handle then peered into the back seat.

"Baby!" she yelled out.

Gin could see the driver was bent forward against the steering wheel, and her heart plummeted. What if she was dead? What if she never got to see her baby again? Why wasn't the baby crying?

She stepped closer, Steph paralyzed in silence beside her.

Carmen jerked on the door handle one more time and then she stepped back, her expression eerily set with the same determination as Phil. They both had a mission. To save that woman and her baby.

Gin felt a sudden surge of admiration. Fire was threatening. People were crying. People were watching. Yet this man, this woman, still pushed on, undeterred by the danger around them.

Carmen jerked at the top button of her shirt, fumbled with a second, then hastily tugged it over her head, leaving Gin to admire those sexy abs. She quickly wrapped her shirt around her arm, stepped forward, and without hesitation, drove her elbow into the window. Once. Twice. With every blow, she ground her teeth. With every blow, she growled in pain.

She threw her weight into the last blow and glass shattered inward. The flames were now shooting out from under the car and crawling up the side of the car.

People yelled out. Urging them to go faster, urging them to get away, Gin wasn't sure. Voices mingled into incoherent sentences.

Carmen fumbled inside, found the latch, and jerked the door open.

She slammed the unlock button. Phil yanked the driver's door open while Carmen leaned into the back seat.

They were in perfect sync with one another, as if reading what the other needed the other to do, setting each other up to get the job done with speed. Was it practice? Was it pure instinct? Gin didn't know, only that it was skilled perfection watching these two in action.

"Pulse!" Phil yelled out.

Gin took in a calming breath.

Out of nowhere, a man ran into action with a fire extinguisher.

Phil secured the woman's head and neck while he pulled her back to a sitting position.

Gin heard the faint sound of groaning and couldn't help but feel another wave of relief.

White foam shot out of the extinguisher as the man squatted beside the car, directing the nozzle beneath the frame.

Smoke billowed around the car until everything went completely out of sight. Phil. The man. Carmen. All gone.

Gin held her breath. Steph squeezed against her, her hand tightening around Gin's arm.

Her date stepped in beside them. What the hell was she still doing here? Was she that desperate? "Are they insane? They're going to get themselves killed trying to play heroes."

With pride, Gin answered. "They are heroes. They're firemen."

And she meant it with the utmost respect. She was witnessing heroes in action. True heroes.

"This is all a little too weird for me. Have a great life, Gin." The date stormed off, and Gin didn't feel bad, didn't even glance at her retreating back.

Time seemed to stand still while Gin strained to see anything through the smoke. The crowd backed away even farther as the smoke seemed to crawl across the ground, toward the sky, completely covering all visibility.

"I'm in love with that man," Steph mumbled beside her. "I think I'm going to marry him."

Gin could well understand the emotional statement. In love, no. She wasn't in love. But damn if she didn't want to fuck that hero one more time. And Carmen had screwed up a date. Again. This was becoming habit for her. A habit she would have to pay for. Soon.

Finally, like a magical being emerging out of the pits of death, Carmen materialized out of the black haze, a baby held tight against her chest.

Awed amazement washed over the crowd through loud cheers and clapping as Carmen stepped onto the curb, that baby cradled in her grasp. It was the sexiest thing Gin had ever seen. Again, her crotch tightened and heat skimmed along her body.

She was going straight to hell for the vivid, naughty pictures weaving with warp speed through her mind. Lust. She was in complete lust.

Phil stepped out of the haze seconds later with a woman limp in his arms. He gently laid her down in the grass and began checking her vitals. Blood covered her face and chest, but she was breathing and would live to love that baby.

The sound of sirens cut through the night and finally, their lights beaconed around the parking lot as they came to a stop behind the silver car.

The paramedics took over the woman's care.

For the first time since the whole ordeal had begun, Carmen looked over to Gin. Lust danced in her eyes. They had unfinished business. Gin couldn't wait to get to it.

Chapter Thirteen

I need your help with this one." Phil nodded toward the first car. "I'm not sure how to handle it. Appears they were, um, sexing and driving?"

Steph giggled.

Phil leaned in and mumbled under his breath. "She's a cop. Several witnesses said she ran the stop sign." He pointed at the intersection.

A woman stepped out of the passenger door of the silver car, dark brown hair tousled, dark blue eyes full of sorrow, blanket wrapped around her body. From beneath the edge, Gin could see she wasn't wearing pants.

"I'm so sorry. Is everyone okay?" the woman cried.

"Get back in the fucking car, Lidia!" a woman shouted from inside.

Gin gasped. She would know that voice anywhere.

Teresa.

Carmen turned to look at Gin with the sound, her head angling, her brow creasing, recognition crawling across her eyes.

Gin took several steps closer, needing to see Teresa's face, to see that embarrassment devouring that cheating bitch's expression.

Steph followed. "Is it her? Please tell me it is."

Gin took several more steps until she could see the driver's face. Teresa. Blood was blotched on her cheek and forehead, but otherwise, she looked unharmed.

She turned to see Gin. A forlorn expression washed over her face. She attempted a smile, then turned away.

"It's her," Gin breathed.

Steph burst out laughing. "Well, if that ain't karma at its finest. Good ole, fuck everybody, anytime, anywhere, Teresa." She nudged Gin. "Told you her day was coming. And today, you get to bear witness to that loser getting what she deserves. Damn, I love karma!"

Gin felt a surge of guilt to be that thrilled with so much destruction around her. Her grandmother was right. Karma would take care of the rest. Oh God, how it was taking care of the rest.

For sure, she would be reprimanded for this. And if there was any alcohol in her system, her own stupidity would take care of the rest. The hero would be stripped of her title. Who knew, maybe she'd get to go work as a rent-a-cop at the bank so she could get her rocks off in a vault on lunch break.

What a loser. What had she ever seen in her?

She knew. Lust had turned her stupid.

Gin recalled Teresa having to jump into action while out on a dinner date in the beginning of their relationship. They'd stopped for gas, which gave Gin an opportunity to buy a candy bar to munch while she finished her erotic novel.

Gin had been on the candy aisle trying to decide between dark chocolate with nuts or caramel with cashews, or both, when she heard the single sentence she thought was only scripted for the movies.

"I have a gun. Give me all the cash in the register."

As Gin registered that those words were real, that there was no TV playing a movie, Teresa moved up behind her.

She pushed her mouth against Gin's ear while giving her arm a firm tug toward the floor. "Get down, Gin. Stay down."

Gin's crotch had throbbed while those lips commanded her, while she was being pushed to the floor. Even with her heart hammering, her insides had throbbed.

Leave it to her to get turned on during a holdup. The same way she was getting turned on during a horrible traffic accident.

The robber was in her view at the end of the aisle. His hand was shoved in his jacket pocket, which was pointed directly at the cashier. Her dark brown eyes were wide with fear, and her bottom lip quivered.

Teresa slipped her hand inside her leather jacket and pulled her gun from the holster she always wore. The same holster that Gin couldn't wait to remove. The same one she eventually got to remove nightly. Daily. Several times if she was lucky. Something about a woman in uniform made her wet with need.

Teresa flipped the safety, slowly rose, and started a quiet prowl down the aisle, her gun leveled toward the floor.

The guy bounced from foot to foot, yelling at the poor woman to move faster, jabbing the gun toward her. He was clearly agitated and impatient and kept glancing out the window to the parking lot.

Teresa reached the end of the aisle while Gin lay flat in paralyzed intrigue. And heated lust. It was the first time she knew for sure that she was in love with Teresa. Until then, she knew there were growing emotions. That her feelings were growing stronger. But until she watched a hero in action, fearless, hot, she hadn't known that she was in love with this woman.

Teresa braced her feet apart and aimed the gun at his back. "Freeze!"

As if he didn't understand the command, or was just plain stupid, the guy turned so fast Gin was positive Teresa was going to shoot him out of reflex alone. Positive she was going to hear the crack of the pistol. Gin would have. Without a doubt, she knew she would have pulled that trigger. She knew that as sure as she knew she needed air to breathe. Instinct to protect her own life would have prevailed before the guy could have twisted his wrist to aim the gun on her.

But not Teresa. She didn't even flinch. She stood rooted, grip firm and sure around the gun, not a single shake in her posture.

"Easy, pal." Teresa finally leveled the muzzle at his head. The guy, no, a kid, a fucking kid, froze. "Don't be stupid tonight."

Gin couldn't breathe. She couldn't move a muscle while she stared at the guy, terrified he would jerk his hand up and pull the trigger. Would Teresa beat him to the draw? She was a trained cop, had probably drawn her weapon more times than anyone could count, had no doubt pulled the trigger just as many times. Would a street kid have that kind of skill? Would Gin bear witness to his final and fatal mistake?

"I need you to slowly pull that hand out of your pocket, kid." Teresa never left her spot, never wavered from her position. "Do it."

"Please. Don't shoot," the guy begged, tears springing to his hazel eyes. "It's not a gun."

"Now!" Teresa barked.

Gin had to squeeze her legs together to ease the burn. It was insane how turned on she was.

The guy shuddered at her command, tears now falling down his cheeks. He held up his free hand and then slowly pulled the other hand from his pocket.

In his grasp was a candy bar.

Gin heaved a sigh of relief. Had Teresa known? Had her experiences warned her that this kid wasn't truly armed? Either way, the moment gave Gin a whole new respect for law enforcement. They put their lives on the line every day in situations just like this one.

"Get on your knees!"

The guy dropped straight down.

Teresa finally darted forward, shoved the guy flat on the floor, twisted his arms behind him, and dropped her knee into his spine while she reached in her pocket for a pair of cuffs.

Gin would never forget that moment. The moment she couldn't wait to get home, to be stripped naked, and cuffed to the bed. Those images had been just as vivid then as the ones that involved Carmen right now.

Sex had been raw and unfiltered that night, sex that included those cuffs. Several times.

Two years later, those emotions had crawled out of her almost the same way they had crawled in. By watching Teresa in action.

Those memories, the cruel way in which their relationship had ended, was the exact reason Gin shouldn't be standing here watching yet another hero in action, with her crotch a wet mess, her insides clenching, and the yearning for one more night strong in her gut.

Yet, this time something was different. Something deeper. The throb she'd felt then was merely a pulse compared to the jabbing throb between her thighs right now.

Teresa's actions had stirred something inside her. Actions that had lead to a reaction. That reaction, that burning need, was what scared her the most right this second. Those reactions seemed to always be triggered by heartfelt emotions. Lust. Admiration. Whatever it was, it could lead to trouble. Had led her to trouble.

It was her weakness for women in uniform.

She'd already been there once, and she damn sure never wanted to go back.

Yet, even with that knowledge that she was being a dumbass once again, she couldn't turn away. Carmen was so fucking hot with sweat glistening on her body, with black smudges across her cheeks and arms, still staring at Gin, reading her with a cocked smile.

With a nod, she turned around and started walking toward Teresa's car.

An hour slid by while more ambulances arrived and started taking care of the victims. Carmen joked around with the kids while Mom and Dad were treated. Dad was placed in the ambulance with Mom and the kids joining. The woman and her baby were carried away in another.

As for Teresa, she was placed on a gurney while a police officer followed. She'd refused a breathalyzer, which proved her guilt in Gin's eyes. Her date, naked beneath her blanket, cried alligator tears the entire time.

When the tow trucks arrived, Gin lost sight of Carmen.

The hero had vanished.

CHAPTER FOURTEEN

Gin couldn't stop the images from replaying in her mind as she took the long way home. She drove down back roads she hadn't visited in years just to absorb the chaos of the night. To absorb her feelings. Her emotions.

Teresa was probably going to jail. She could possibly lose her job. Almost surely, she would lose her job. Gin shouldn't be happy about that, but she was. Teresa abused her title. Used her position to score women.

Thoughts of Carmen squeezed in once again. The image of her perched on her favorite stool, waiting. Was she any different from Teresa? Was that firehouse T-shirt the same as a badge?

Why didn't it feel the same? Was she simply giving excuses because she wanted to fuck her again?

And here she was, those thoughts, those desires, of Carmen, crowding inside her mind again. A need squirming to life. A want nuzzling deep.

What was wrong with her? Couldn't she find a normal relationship? Couldn't she lust after a normal person?

Not like her date tonight who tossed out sweet comments like candy from a float in a Christmas parade. The real kind. The kind you could read in someone's eyes. When they meant it. When there wasn't an ulterior motive behind the words.

She was so sick of finding the same kind of women. The ones who were looking for notches without enough brassy balls to say that out loud.

Unlike Carmen who hadn't hesitated to announce her motives. To fuck and never look back.

She'd laid out those facts for Gin to take or leave.

God, she'd taken them. Wanted to take them again. Right now.

Fuck. She was twisted and couldn't even blame sexual deprivation anymore.

Carmen had taken great care of that little issue as well.

The images bloomed once again. Carmen running into danger without an ounce of fear. There'd been smoke. There'd been a fire. There'd been screaming. Carmen had barged onward like a trained soldier without a weapon. She had been her own weapon to dismantle destruction.

Fuck. It had been so hot. Too hot. Too fucking hot.

It was sick of her, but it was the hottest thing she'd ever witnessed. Seeing Teresa braced for the kill shot was nothing compared to watching Carmen half naked, breaking glass with her own body. Barking orders, the hood slide like a pro to get to the other side of the car, and for crying out loud, there was nothing hotter than a hero carrying a baby against her chest.

Gin was going straight to hell for the naughty thoughts. No other direction but down for a girl who wanted to fuck another person while people cried in fear and in pain around her. Straight to hell. Straight...down.

Even her date storming away, bristled and scorned, like the whole episode was some sort of sick joke, hadn't dragged her sights away from the scene of Carmen in action.

She was a true hero, to the pit of her soul, and Gin felt honored to have witnessed every minute of her fearlessness.

There was only one blemish in the finale of the night. She was going home alone with so many dirty thoughts twisted into her conscious, no matter how much she tried to drive them away along these back roads. As sick as the notion was, she wanted Carmen.

Again. Tonight. One more time. She deserved as much. Carmen had ruined her date, after all.

Finally, Gin decided the drive was useless. She should go home, write another redundant article, and take her horny ass to bed with her handy vibrator. Tonight, it would have to do.

Gin pulled down her driveway, her crotch a wet mess, and felt the breath catch in her chest like a thick wool at the sight of Carmen leaning against her car in front of the garage doors.

The images that had only seconds ago dominated her mind blossomed into scalding reality.

She couldn't help herself. She shouldn't want any part of Carmen. Hero or not. Hot or not. She stood for everything Gin could never have in her life. Her lifestyle was against all of her morals.

Carmen was always the single one in the group, women pining for her attention, like the instructor at the bakery. Carmen was always going to be that woman. Always eager for that attention. Eager to take action with the attention.

The headlights flicked across Carmen's body, once again wrapped inside her button-up shirt, and suddenly Gin no longer cared about her morals. Not tonight. Not after the wicked hot scenes she'd witnessed with her very own eyes.

Tonight, she was going to fuck and be fucked by Carmen again. Hopefully followed by a few more times. She couldn't say no to that open invitation if her business, her future, maybe even her life, depended on it.

Gin parked the car as slowly as possible when she really wanted to slam the brake, drive the shifter into park, and throw herself into those arms.

She stepped out of the car as calmly as possible when so much need was bottled up inside and turned to find Carmen beside the door.

"I'm sorry about your date." Carmen didn't appear sorry at all. A smile lingered at the corner of her lips. "And Teresa."

Gin had no desire to think about Teresa another second, let alone talk about her. She wanted to be naked, crushed against Carmen, an orgasm ripped from her body.

"No, you're not," Gin whispered.

Carmen stepped forward and closed the door behind Gin. "You're right."

She pinned Gin against the car. Her mouth came down hard against Gin's.

Gin moaned and draped her arms around Carmen's neck. She arched into her, greedy, desperate for penetration, to feel their skin against each other.

Carmen pulled back, her lips damp. "No matter how many arms you put around me, you won't be rescued tonight, sexy."

She hiked the dress up Gin's legs, giving no thought to neighbors possibly looking out their windows, palmed her ass, then drew her up and around her hips.

"Steph is a blabbermouth." Gin captured those lips again while Carmen started for the front door.

She sat Gin down at the threshold so she could fumble with keys, a lock, a knob, all while Carmen nibbled her neck, her fingers in the alcove of Gin's thighs.

They shoved through the door and immediately started tugging and ripping at clothes, both eager for skin contact.

Long minutes later, Gin flattened her face against the tile wall of the shower while Carmen bit down on her shoulder, and buried her fingers deep inside Gin from behind.

Gin gasped, drawing in heated breaths. She eased onto the tips of her toes, her body jolting and cramping and so fucking alive, with every thrust of Carmen's lean hips.

No other time in her life, in bed, out of bed, in love, out of love, had she felt this electrified. Her nerves hummed. Her skin tingled. Her insides felt like bowstrings, ready to spring at any second.

Worse, Carmen knew. She had a wicked way of pushing Gin right to the edge, to that place where the blistering hot need was nothing more than a fall away, and then slowly, easily, steadily, pulling her back from the abyss.

Over. Over. Over again, she kept Gin from falling, yet kept her so close to that glorious release it was mind-blowing.

Like right now. Dammit. Gin feared Carmen was going to drive her mad. Thrusts slowing from their rapid beat, that finger that was only seconds ago flicking and teasing her clit, was now barely a touch.

"Fucking finish me!" Gin barked and let her head fall backward to Carmen's shoulder. "Please," she whispered.

Carmen smiled against her cheek. "I was wrong about you." She drove her fingers inside Gin, once again climbing into a steady rhythm. "You do beg."

She flicked Gin's clit, biting her neck, then kissing away the sting.

Gin ground her teeth together as the pressure built, her insides tightening around those pleasing fingers, and she came in a brilliant flash of white light.

She clawed at Carmen's thighs while her insides convulsed and spasmed, her cries of gratified release erotic against her own ears, her body rocking and arching and coming until she was utterly depleted. With a whimper, she sagged into Carmen's strong embrace.

Carmen opened the shower door and lifted Gin easily into her arms then carried her to the bed. She kneed Gin's legs apart and slowly ground into her. Drops of water slipped down the strands of her hair and fell onto Gin's cheek.

She stared down for several agonizing seconds, something Gin didn't recognize flashing in those eyes, before she captured Gin's lips and snaked her tongue inside.

Trouble. Gin smelled trouble. Felt it to the pit of her core. It came from her chest, like a fluttering of wings. Like a twitch. She'd felt that before. That desire. That need. That aching want.

She'd never forget what that feeling was like. How it had consumed her. How she'd leapt into it without a single hesitation. She would never forget because it eventually tore her world apart in the form of a cheater. In the form of a hero. A hero who was beloved and idolized by so many. A hero. A fucking hero had ripped her heart in half. A hero who was hopefully locked behind bars this very minute.

And here was another one, who had already made her intentions clear, making her feel something, too much, everything, all over again.

This wasn't supposed to happen. Couldn't happen. She refused to feel anything. Not a sputter. Not a twitch. Not even a knot.

Never again. Never again. Never again.

She pushed against Carmen until she rolled onto her back.

Carmen sensed the shift of mood almost immediately. Gin straddled her hips and ground down over her pelvic bone. Her expression was hard. Determined. As much as it knotted her stomach knowing that the next time she saw Gin, they would pretend tonight never happened, that weeks ago hadn't happened, she was thankful. Gin wasn't going to let her in. She wasn't going to allow her beliefs, her morals, the fence around that heart, to be penetrated. She wasn't going to break her own rules.

Carmen didn't want in. She didn't want to break the links in the chain that Gin used to protect herself. Besides, she didn't have the necessary tools for such a conquest. That kind of battle required love.

Work. Women. Always and forever in that exact order.

Hours later, Carmen stared down into Gin's sleeping face, listening to her steady breath, soaking in the normalcy of the moment. Not a single time in her life had she ever felt this connected. This content. This relaxed.

Those emotions, the ones creeping inside right now, were forbidden. Not only were they forbidden, they were also foreign to her. Her heart didn't sputter like it was right now. Her stomach didn't knot the way it was right now. And her life didn't feel empty, the way it felt right now.

After several more minutes absorbing their time together, soaking in their time that had finally come to a conclusion, Carmen wiggled from beneath Gin's sensual weight.

She dressed slowly while looking back, unconsciously willing Gin to wake, to stop her, to call her back to the bed, to beg her one more time with that rushed whisper.

Gin didn't wake up. She didn't even move.

Just as well. Carmen didn't belong here. Didn't belong in that bed. Didn't belong in Gin's life. Worse, Gin knew it, too.

Before Gin woke up and did exactly what Carmen wanted her to do, what she shouldn't want her to do, she left the room and let herself out the front door. She couldn't give Gin the opportunity to poke her ego again.

It was bruised enough already.

Chapter Fifteen

Carmen shucked out of her boots and leaned against the ladder truck. For six hours, she and her crew had been fighting a warehouse fire. Thankfully, the employees inside had been nearby when the fire ignited and were able to get everyone out of the building.

Problem was, for the first time in her life, including her time as a volunteer fireman at sixteen, when just being near a fire should have set her nerves on edge, Carmen had hesitated upon entry. Firemen never hesitated. She never hesitated. It wasn't, nor had it ever been, in her nature to hesitate.

She was a beast. Unafraid of the unknown. Unafraid of anything. Yet today, she'd stalled.

It made her mad. Lives depended on her. Her own life, and those of her colleagues, depended on her willingness to drive into the danger with a clear head. With a clear mind. To conquer. To protect. Today, the hesitation had come naturally.

What if she didn't make it back out? What if today was the day the curse came to snatch her away? Who would care? Phil? Her brothers and sisters of the firehouse? It was their job to care. Their integrity. Their unwavering respect.

But who, beyond the firehouse, would miss her? Her mother. Sure. That was without question. But who else?

Romantically, she loved no one. And no one loved her in return. There would be no one to fall to their knees in tears over her casket.

No one to pluck a rose from the arrangement splayed across her casket like her mother had done at her father's funeral.

She didn't have that kind of love in her life. She'd chosen the path to protect someone's heart. But during the seconds she'd stalled outside the warehouse door, she'd mourned for a person who didn't exist. The notion that no one beyond the men and women she worked with, beyond the mother who gave birth to her, cared about her. She would be nothing more than a plaque on a fire station wall.

It was sad, really. Even if being alone was her choice.

Now, pressed against the truck, she was angry at herself. A beast didn't stall. A warrior didn't think. A hero never hesitated.

She barely spoke to anyone as she moved robotically through the rest of her shift. She showered, dressed, duffel bag in hand, same as every shift, and then headed out to her car.

Minutes ticked by while she sat behind the wheel, watching her fellow firefighters walk out, joshing each other, some scurrying to their cars in haste to get home to loved ones, like Daniel, who all but ran across the parking lot.

She loved them all. Would protect them with her life. Would give her life if it meant saving theirs. But today, could she have said that? Today, had she given her all?

No. She hadn't.

Worse, she couldn't stop thinking about the fires. How the inspectors still hadn't raised the red flag. Hers was flying high. Screaming that something was wrong. Yet, she had no one to tell. No one to smack her back in line, like Phil. He was in love. Spending every free minute with Steph.

Carmen didn't want to disrupt his happiness with a gut feeling.

But she couldn't shake it either. It was eating at her.

With a grunt, she cranked the car and headed toward the old bookstore. She'd driven by there almost every day on her way to work. The warning tape had already been disturbed, most of it lying across the grounds.

She could just take a peek. Maybe walk around the yard. Then maybe she would get rid of this ridiculous notion that there was an arsonist planning his next move out there somewhere.

After spotting several fresh beer bottles lying beside the front door and on the walkway, Carmen was positive the place was once again being used for a hangout. The investigators, if they'd come at all, were surely done with the building, with their inspections.

The doors had been kicked in the day of the fire. Only one piece of warning tape remained across the entrance.

Carmen ducked under and entered. "Fire department! If anyone's in here, you need to vacate the premises. You're trespassing."

She waited for several seconds, but there were no sounds other than the creaking beneath her own feet.

The air smelled like burned wood, like a recently distinguished campfire. A scent she'd become accustomed to over the years. A scent she rather liked. Not from burned buildings, but from campfires.

She hadn't been on a camping trip in years and made a mental note to see if any of the guys might want to get a trip planned.

It had been too long since she relaxed on a weekend, fished by a lazy river, drank a beer beneath the stars.

She needed the downtime. Time to step away and just breathe.

A thought fluttered through her conscious. She and Gin in a tent, naked and whimpering and fucking, beneath a night sky clear and full of twinkling yellow lights.

With a growl, she shook her head. For crying out loud, why couldn't she get her shit together?

She started her inspection closest to the most burned part of the building, a part of the wall that was beneath a vaulted ceiling. If she recalled, there had been a spiral staircase in that location many years ago that led to the top floor, probably the naughty sections, where the lesbian and gay books would have been tucked in the farthest corner of the room, if there had been any at all.

The place had been closed for many years and that staircase likely dismantled from age or removed by an antiquer. There was no other visible route to that top floor, but the open ceiling would have given plenty of fuel to the fire below. If she was going to start a fire, she would have done it in that exact spot. The air from the open floor plan above would have fueled the fire quickly.

But only a more skilled arsonist would know that. An amateur would have likely started in a corner, probably used matches or gasoline, something easily detectable. The inspectors hadn't found anything suspicious. So far, neither had she.

Among the debris, she didn't see anything that would be considered evidence. Just trash and cigarette packs and empty beer bottles. Nothing to start a fire.

She scanned the rest of the room. Two open doorways led into another room to her left. An old desk was against the wall between those openings. Carmen could see emptiness beyond the threshold.

To the right, the exact same layout except for the loft that would have looked down into that opening from the top floor.

On the left, she spotted two doors that hadn't been removed or burned, and she walked across the room to the first one. A closet. Empty. No entrance up or down. Not even attic access.

Behind the other door was a staircase that led into a basement. She didn't recall any of the other firemen going in or out of this door. Possibly the inspectors had been down there during their walk-through.

She cautiously started down, narrowing her eyes into the dimness, until she got to the floor. Heaps of debris littered the cement floor and corners, and the acrid scent of urine struck her.

With her hand covering her nose, she kicked bottles and cups and pizza boxes to the side as she made her way toward the doorway that led beneath the room where the fire had been started.

The air was more breathable in the next room. Windows toward the top of the brick wall had been busted out, and glass sparkled along the floor as she moved deeper inside the room.

A metal bin was in the center, no doubt where the homeless built a fire for warmth.

She spotted charred brick in several locations around the room and moved closer to inspect.

At first glance, the charred spots on the brick appeared to be from idiots who might have started their own campfire, not wanting to share or stand by the safer one in the center. But as she moved closer, she realized that wasn't the cause.

There were burn marks in the floor and about two or three feet of charred bricks reaching up the wall. Someone could have started a fire there for warmth, no doubt, but it didn't make sense when the barrel in the middle of the room would have offered ample heat. Nor was there any kind of ring around the blackened spots to prove they had intended to contain the fire. So close to the brick wall, on a concrete floor, they would have had to continually feed paper into it to keep it going.

No. That wasn't the reason.

She moved to another spot. Same thing. Burned floor. Charred bricks leading several feet up the wall. Another spot, this one darker, showed the same results except the charred marks led a little higher. The location that would have been beneath where the fire started was the darkest, smoke marks led even higher, although they never reached high enough to touch the ceiling above her.

She turned in a slow circle to take in all the areas, from the lighter, more aged ones to more recent, more blackened spots.

An amateur. He'd been practicing. Right here in this basement, he'd been testing himself, testing his limits, testing the results. The evidence was all around her.

Excitement rolled through her. She'd known it all along. That something wasn't right. That her gut had been warning her, nudging her conscious to listen.

Now what? If she called her chief, he'd be pissed that she was inspecting all alone, which also screamed that she didn't trust the fire inspectors. If she called Phil, he would rush to her side, which would get them both in trouble and possibly reprimanded.

She couldn't have that eating at her, especially when he was well on his way to wedding bells.

Daniel. He was her captain. And a damn good one. He'd always teased her when he caught her casually inspecting the fire area, the surrounding wreckage, told her she was in the wrong line of work. It was his job to listen. And to handle the situation.

She pulled out her cell phone and dialed him. He would know what to do. He would know what the next step was.

As the ring tone began, another emotion snaked inside. Home. This spot in a basement, inspecting filth and debris, finding results, finding proof, felt like home. Like inspecting was where she was meant to be.

If only she hadn't been groomed to be a fireman for the rest of her life. If only she weren't destined to follow in her daddy's footsteps. If only she could branch off from her own family tree.

If only.

Daniel answered the phone. "What's up, Maverick?"

"I found something. I need your help." Carmen rushed the words before she chickened out.

Two hours later, she pulled away from the curb with a smile. Daniel had taken care of everything. Come to her rescue. Come to inspect and arrived at the same conclusion. He'd even called the chief and kept Carmen out of the conversation for now. He clapped her on the back, congratulated her, then reminded her that he always knew she secretly yearned to do the gritty work.

Right now, her yearning was for Delaney's. Sex. A sexy woman to grind beneath her.

She was going to have a beer. She wasn't going to glance over her shoulder in hopes of seeing if Gin or her posse showed up. She wouldn't look, because she didn't care. Weeks had crawled by since her last night with Gin. The last night that was still burning in her mind.

A night she needed to fill with something fresh. She needed that fresh meat to shove out the thoughts.

She and Gin were both on a different course in life. Gin to find her happy ever after, even if she would never find it if she didn't open her heart to it. Carmen possibly to never find that kind of happiness, because she couldn't open her heart for it.

It was what it was. They were both big girls. They would eventually find their own paths in this thing called life. They both would be okay. She knew that.

But tonight, she was going to find a woman to wipe away those wicked thoughts. She was going to perch herself on her favorite stool, closest to the front door, where, exactly as Gin had put it, she could have first choice of whoever walked through that door.

She'd gotten herself off course. Tonight, with fresh, new excitement of possibly reaching further into this inspection world, she was going to get herself back on track. That was all. Gin had shoved her off track, and it was time to get herself back on it.

Sex was going to help her do just that.

CHAPTER SIXTEEN

A re you sure this is a good idea?" Gin asked Phil and Steph while she scanned the interior of Delaney's. "Having the date here?"

Her date was due in the next thirty minutes. Officially, number twenty-three. A date Steph had arranged. Only three more dates and she could call this project a wrap.

In the past few weeks, she could have knocked out every last one. She'd gotten several promising invitations. But something had been nagging at her, and she simply hadn't been in the mood to date. Not even for a paycheck that wouldn't keep her from sinking. Fact was, the fight was all but over. She knew it. Her heart knew it. Had known it all along. Now the time had come to take action. Time to shit or get off the pot, so to speak.

Not to mention the articles were a joke. Every word, every paragraph, and every minute she put into writing them was just as much a waste of her time as the dates were. She hadn't gotten any closer to finding someone who made her heart flutter than Patricia had gotten to accepting the f-bomb in her articles.

As for the real world, it was time to call in the professionals. First thing Monday morning, she'd make that dreaded call to the only mechanic she knew who specialized in classics. They would send a wrecker and haul that beauty off to the shop. From there, she would be forced to wait. What had made it stop running? Was it fixable? Was that fix simple or would she have to sell body parts to cover the bill? If the original engine couldn't be repaired, would the car still be worth the value? Would the collector still want the car? With the same price tag?

Too many questions.

She prayed the repair would be simple. Something she'd overlooked after all this time.

With every ounce of her being, she wanted Mr. Thornton to own that car. He was a great guy who not only collected specific antiques, he treasured them. The car deserved to be treasured, especially from someone who thought so fondly of her grandparents. He was without a doubt the best person to take over ownership of such a priceless possession.

Monday, the hell of her future could begin. But tonight, she was going to get this date over with and then she was going to drive home, get naked, climb in bed with her computer, and ride her vibrator until all thoughts and worries vanished.

"It's the perfect place. Far better than a bakery," Phil said.

"Speaking of, did you see Teresa's mug shot in the paper?" Steph cooed. "Local cop arrested for DUI. Makes me so happy."

Of course Gin had seen it. It had made her smile. Teresa had finally gotten what she deserved. Karma had finally found her.

But that wasn't what was on her mind today.

Carmen was. She glanced toward the front door. What she should have asked Phil was, would Carmen be pissed that she had used her personal space to get the data for another article. To search for something, someone, to shift her heart out of rhythmic sequence.

This was Carmen's house. Her place. Her stool. Her friends. Her co-workers. It felt wrong, somehow. But Steph had insisted. Pleaded, in fact. Truthfully, she didn't want to see Carmen again. She didn't think straight when she was around her. Near her. For sure, when Carmen was inside her.

Weeks had now passed since she awoke to the bed empty beside her. Without Carmen's heat pressing against her. Lying there in her arms had felt so natural. She'd never been so peaceful.

She still hadn't concluded if those emotions had stemmed from being with someone who would protect her even if they disliked her.

She'd watched Carmen do exactly that with a total stranger. Protect them. It had been so hot.

However, she'd felt the same ease when she was with Teresa, who slept with her gun inches from her head. Another Velcroed beneath several end tables. And yet another by each door in a fake floating shelf. Gin had never slept so soundly knowing Teresa would go into assassin mode with a faint noise.

Except she couldn't protect Gin's heart. In fact, she'd been the one who had broken it. Dirtbag. A dirtbag who was now in the same detention center as the scum she'd arrested. Oh, what fun she must be having. The bitch would probably drop the soap on purpose.

"I do believe you're enjoying the buddy system far more than a man should." Gin elbowed Phil, trying to clear her thoughts. "We may have to make you an honorary member."

The front door opened and Gin turned to find Carmen stepping inside. Fuck. Fuck. Fuck. Her stomach knotted so hard it choked her breath. This was exactly what she'd been worried about. Her reaction to Carmen. Dammit.

No. She didn't have a reaction to Carmen. These emotions, the freaking spasm of wings, were nothing more than the uncertainty of Carmen's reaction to the game, to her date, being played out in her territory. That's all it was. God knew she couldn't feel something deeper for a woman she despised.

Carmen stopped cold when she saw Phil, Steph, and Gin perched at the bar. She groaned. What the hell were they doing here? And did Gin have to look so sexy in her tight blue jeans and loose almost see-through button-up blouse?

She shouldn't want her so bad. Shouldn't be affected by the sight of her. No matter how much she wanted to deny their chemistry, it existed. She hated that. The existence of something she'd fought so hard for so long to never have. It was wrong. On so many levels, it was wrong.

Not to mention she was on another high. A high stemmed from finding proof that the bookstore fire had been deliberately started. That an arsonist was walking among them. That the inspectors would be called back to the scene and questioned about not doing their job to the fullest.

Of course, she didn't want anyone to get in trouble, but something had kept them from walking down a simple flight of steps. The fires could have already been flagged as suspicious and the investigation to find the creep could possibly be over.

With a struggle, she let the door close behind her. She forced one foot in front of the other as she made her way to the bar. To her stool. To her perch. Bypassing several women who gave admiring coos in her quest to appear normal.

"What's up?" she asked Phil, trying to sound casual while so many raw images flashed through her mind.

"I set Gin up on a blind date tonight. A hot, single contractor who has been doing work in my office building this week." Steph grinned although there was a hint of mischief behind the smile.

"We get front row seats to the buddy system again tonight," Phil added. "Let's hope it doesn't end the same way as the bakery disaster." He included a smirk. "Although those kids you invited to the station were cool. I may want kids just like them one day." He looked at Steph who offered a sweet smile.

Sheesh. Were these two going to make out all night? It was cute how they were head over heels but rather unnerving when Carmen just wanted to find a woman, take her out of here, and fuck all night.

Carmen turned her sights on Gin, praying it would end exactly the same way, minus the collision, with Teresa still going to jail. It gave her pleasure to know that Gin had gotten even a little bit of closure, that she'd gotten to watch karma in action. She needed the night to also include Gin's erotic cries against her mouth. No. Dammit. She didn't. "Cool. Good luck."

"See, I told you Carmen was fine with it." Steph waved a hand toward Gin. "This is the perfect place."

But it wasn't. Not here. Of all places they could have chosen, this was the worst one. Slow anger bubbled as Gin turned up her beer, her expression blank, like a person who was nothing more than a casual friend. Definitely not from a person who had been beneath her, screaming her name, several times before.

"I agree. Delaney's is the perfect place," Carmen lied.

Why did it bother her so much to see someone doing exactly what she had come here with all intentions to do? Move on. Gin had moved on. Their time together had been pushed out of her mind. Her expression said as much. Shit. Why was it eating her alive? Isn't this what she did? Just keep walking? Become friends who nod in passing? Yes. That's exactly what she did. So why the hell was that uncaring expression pissing her off so bad?

"Speaking of dates, I think you have a fan." Gin nodded toward one of the women who had moved aside for Carmen on her path to the stool. "She's cute. Don't let her go to waste." With a wink, she turned her bottle up and downed the remainder of the contents. She placed the empty bottle on the counter and took in a deep breath.

Steph reached over. "Girl, you are buttoned up too tight." She plucked open another button, and the material fell to the side to display the top of her cleavage. "There. Perfect. Don't you think so, Carmen? Phil?"

Before Carmen could protest or even comment on the display of such delectable skin, Phil shook his head. "No way in hell you're dragging me into this mosh pit of doghouses."

Steph laughed and kissed him. "You're adorable. And so you know, you can always look. You just can't touch without losing body parts. I'm easy like that." She added a wicked Joker smile.

The front door opened again, and they all turned to see a woman who was no doubt Gin's date stepping inside. Tall, broad, with the most delicious biceps Gin had ever laid eyes on. Well, not completely true. Not true at all. Carmen's were rather perfect. Not too big. Definitely not too small. And strong. But strong in a hold Gin down and fuck her kind of way.

Steph tugged on Gin's elbow, yanking her out of her heated thoughts, and whispered, "That's her! Isn't she perfect?"

Gin watched Carmen's jaw clench as she watched the date make her way through the women closest to the door. Was she jealous? She couldn't be. Shouldn't be. They had both made their intentions clear. Hadn't they?

"Who needs a gym when you have a construction site? Holy hell! Would you look at those guns," Phil mumbled.

Gin turned her attention back to the woman passing the group at the dartboard. Some of them had offered flirtatious oohs and aahs as Carmen had passed, but the blonde still held her sights on Carmen.

Wasn't that typical? Of course Carmen still held the woman's attention. Like she held many others just like this one. Before the night was over, she would leave with the blonde on her arm. She would explain how she couldn't commit to anything serious, that she was only looking for a good time, and maybe they would cross paths some other time. Then they would fuck.

That's the way Carmen handled life.

The way she would always handle life.

With her head held high, with determination to see this through, to watch Carmen carry on with life the way she was going to do, Gin licked her lips. It was time to move on. Time for both of them to move on.

"Fuck me blind," Gin hissed under her breath, hoping she sounded convincing. "I love you so much, Steph."

Gin moved away to go greet her date, and it was all the strength Carmen could muster not to yank her back.

She didn't want Gin going on this date. Not any date. But especially this date. Good Lord, the woman could throw Gin around like a flimsy rag doll. It was unnerving how jealous she was right now. Emotions ripped through her as Gin smiled up at the woman and led them to a high-top table.

The blonde was still staring at Carmen.

With a grunt, Carmen turned back around.

"Here we go." Steph took a quick sip of her beer and settled her weight against the counter.

"Not sure the buddy system will be required tonight. Looks like Gin is awestruck," Phil said.

Carmen motioned for the bartender, then ordered a beer. She had a feeling she was going to need more than one tonight. Not even the sight of a beautiful woman flirting with her was easing the knot pinching her gut.

"Never judge a book by its cover," Steph said while she intently watched the couple. "The bigger they are, the harder they fall. Although I have dibs on Gin falling. Flat on her back." She added a snort for good measure.

Carmen clamped her teeth together and muscled her self-control not to turn around. Not to shove away from this stool and drag Gin from the bar. On her back is exactly where she wanted Gin.

"I thought that only applied to football and bullies." Phil nuzzled Steph's neck.

Carmen lost the battle and glanced over her shoulder while Phil and Steph giggled like teenagers. Gin was transfixed by her date. It appeared the date was just as spellbound. Their stools were closer, and they were leaning in close to each other.

Gin threw her head back and laughed. The date took the opportunity to take a glance at Gin's cleavage.

Carmen turned around and took a long swallow. The cool malt did little to smother her discomfort.

What, exactly, was she so upset about? The fact that Gin had brought her date here? The fact that Steph had arranged it all? The fact that she was moving on as if Carmen had never existed? The fact that she was enjoying herself so immensely? Or the fact that Carmen was uncomfortable with all of the above?

Whatever the reason, she couldn't draw the anger back in. She wasn't a jealous person. She didn't play games. She had no problem fucking and walking away. So what the hell was wrong? Because the tables had been turned? Because her ego was getting pounded like a boxer's speed bag?

"What do you think about Gin's date, Carmen?" Steph poked Carmen's arm. "Do I know how to pick 'em or what?"

Carmen wanted to scream at her to let Gin find her own damn dates. To mind her own business.

Instead, she shrugged. "If that gawdy bodybuilder look is Gin's type, sure." She took another sip in an attempt to restrain her next words. The cool liquid felt useless to tighten her tongue. "In my experience, muscles that big are for nothing more than showboating. No real worth in them."

Steph threw Phil a look, and Carmen realized the jealousy she'd been feeling had just slipped out.

"She's right." Phil jumped on the defense, forgetting he had only a minute ago bragged about those biceps. "We've watched some just as big, just as built, go spiraling down during training."

A devious smile crept across Steph's lips. "I bet my best friend could find a few good uses for those guns." She looked back to the table. "Shit, even I can think of a few good ways to put those muscles to use."

"Hey now!" Phil barked and drew Steph in for a kiss. "You better watch it, woman."

Fifteen, twenty minutes, slid by while Carmen nursed her second beer, while Steph continued to boast about herself, how she might have found Gin's forever after, periodically hugging Phil because they just couldn't stop touching each other. Carmen refused to look again. If she could refuse to listen, she would have.

What felt like forever passed by, and finally, Steph straightened and said, "We have action, ladies and gentlemen."

Phil glanced over his shoulder while Carmen fought the urge to do the same. Whatever was happening behind her, was none of her business. Absolutely none of her concern.

"She's just going to the bathroom," Phil mumbled.

Relief washed over Carmen. Relief that shouldn't be required. What the hell was happening to her?

Steph stared at him like he'd lost his mind. "Have I not taught you anything?" Her sights moved away from him and back to the table. "Shit. There she goes, following Gin. Don't let me down, Shawn."

Shawn. Even her name sounded tough.

Carmen couldn't resist. She looked up to find the date following close behind Gin, bathroom bound. Even her body language was smug. Arms to the side, tall, proud.

Fucker!

"What am I missing?" Phil asked. "Don't women always go in packs to the bathroom?" He turned to Carmen. "Right?"

Steph looked around him and pleaded with Carmen. "Can you explain it to him?"

"I'm so lost," Phil said. "Is this a gay thing?"

The green-eyed monster roared deep down inside Carmen. "Friends go in packs. Lovers go alone."

"Exactly," Steph added with a tap of her fingers against the counter.

"No shit? So, they're…? Here? In *there*?" He cackled. "Your best friend is a naughty *beast*. Get it, Gin." He snapped his finger in a pitiful attempt at a z formation.

Carmen controlled the urge to push him off the stool. Only one of two things was going to happen with those two behind closed doors. Gin had been practically drooling on herself. The date was just as intrigued with Gin. No way sex wouldn't happen. Right here. In her bar. Her place. Her house.

Why in hell did she give a shit? Gin was free to date, fuck, love, whoever she wanted. So was Carmen. Why, goddamn, why, was it eating her alive to imagine what was happening inside a bathroom stall?

"I'm so happy you're a sexual decrepit." Steph kissed Phil hard on the cheek.

"I have no idea what that means, but I am proud, and maybe, no, not maybe, for sure a little confused why I'm proud to say I'm so happy it makes you happy." He pulled her against his stool and kissed her again.

Minutes passed by while Carmen sucked at the contents of her bottle. She needed to grab the blonde who was still laughing with her friends at the dartboard and make her exit. A long night of sweaty sex would yank Gin from her mind, who had no place being in her head to begin with. Maybe that would work. Probably not. No way in hell. Not right now while her anger and confusion were whiplashing.

The longer the clock ticked, the antsier she became. The bottle was soon empty. She needed another. She didn't want another. What she really wanted to do was bust up the sexual show happening in that damn bathroom.

As if hailed by her mental anger, Gin emerged from the bathroom, followed closely by her date. Carmen willed Gin to look at her, though she didn't know why. Yes. She did. She wanted Gin to see the disappointment in her eyes.

Gin passed their stools without a single glance, but the date had a point to prove.

She tagged Carmen in a steady stare, wiped the corners of her mouth, and winked.

The noise of the bar, the TV, the clatter of balls from the pool table, the laughter from the group at the dartboard, the live band playing toward the back of the room, faded in the distance as the anger ruptured along her nerves. Her ears rang as the date passed them by.

"Here we go," Steph breathed, pulling Carmen out of her dying need to body slam the woman.

Phil was practically on the edge of his seat watching the scene unfold. "What are we watching for?"

"For Gin to tell us if this hottie is a scumbag, a true gentleman, or the one she's been waiting for," Steph said.

"And she got all that information in one trip to a bathroom?" Phil uttered.

Steph pulled his head around and kissed him on the cheek again. "You are precious."

Carmen was beyond caring if Gin or her buff date saw her watching. She turned around completely on her stool. She wanted Gin to notice that she was noticing. Dear God, if only she knew why she wanted Gin to notice. It was absolutely foolish of her to be this jealous.

Gin reached into her purse and pulled out a pack of cigarettes.

Carmen's heart lurched in her chest. The after-sex cigarette.

"Gin doesn't smoke. Is that the signal?" Phil asked.

"Yes, she does," Carmen mumbled while Gin tapped a cigarette from the pack.

She'd shared that cigarette. That after-sex cigarette. Damn, she wanted to share one again. No. No, she didn't. She wanted Gin to be too boneless to smoke one. She wanted her in a sexual coma from a night of dirty sex.

The images ripped through her mind, and she clenched her jaw.

"She doesn't, except for…" Steph began. "It's kind of a signal. But not because she needs saving. It's her way of saving herself. Sort of. Kind of. It's a long story." Steph attempted an explanation.

"I'm so lost." Phil threw his hands up.

"You'll see, sweetheart." Steph patted his leg.

Gin put the cigarette to her lips, flipped the lighter over in her fingers, cut her gaze on Carmen, her green eyes narrowing as if she was trying to read something in Carmen's expression. Finally, she winked and lit the tip.

Carmen had seen enough. She shoved off the stool and barged for the front door, bypassing the blonde without a second glance.

Once on the sidewalk, she paced in front of her car, unsure where to go, where to turn, what to do now that she was free of the show, trying to pull her uncharacteristic emotions back in.

Never, ever, had she been so disturbed by anything. Not blood. Not broken bones. Not even the death of a fellow firefighter. Not a single goddamn time.

Right now, she could punch the face of this brick wall and feel nothing. She was that mad. And didn't even know why.

She was more disturbed by her reaction. This wasn't in her character. No drama. No games. No jealousy. It made life easy. So why the hell was she standing on a sidewalk ready to throat punch someone? Hell, she didn't really like Gin enough to feel this much rage.

The front door opened and Gin's date stormed out. She made no eye contact as she barreled toward the end of the parking lot and disappeared around the corner.

Relief flooded Carmen. Far heavier than it should have. This raw emotion was so foreign to her, she didn't know what to make of it, what to do with it, how to even react to it.

What she did know, was that Gin was now dateless inside that bar and from the fact that her date had just left her behind, obviously the date hadn't gone as great as Carmen thought.

A car peeled away in the distance, and Carmen could breathe once again. She inhaled and tried to clear her mind. But there was nothing to clear. She knew exactly where her next steps would lead her. Directly into the bar, to Gin, and without asking permission, she was going to take her out. Take her home. And then take her. Over and over and over again.

The front door opened again, and Gin stepped outside.

She glanced around, spotted Carmen, and headed for her. "Hey, friend. Did the douche leave yet?"

The words, the meaning behind them, that she hadn't just fucked her date in a bathroom stall, deflated Carmen's anger.

Carmen took two steps to get to Gin. With eagerness to touch her, she wrapped her arm around Gin's waist and tugged her forward. She didn't think. She just did it. Kissed her. Hard. Claiming and possessive.

When she drew back, she immediately missed the softness of those plump lips. "Why'd you run the douche off, *friend*?"

Gin gave her a smirk and tightly shook her head. "That word has a fake feel to it considering we bypassed that zone by leaps and bounds. Not to mention, I don't even like you." She angled her head and studied Carmen. "Benefits. This is simply benefits. Without friendship. Deal?"

Carmen gave a stiff nod. She didn't want to be friends, either. She wanted permanent benefits. For the first time in her life, she wanted something permanent.

"Speaking of dates, why'd you leave your could-be fuck behind? She was cute."

"Wasn't my type." Carmen pushed a lock of hair behind Gin's ear simply to do something with her hand. Gin was her type. The woman who didn't like her. The very one in her grasp who would be naked against her body before the end of this night. Again. "So what was wrong with this date? Thought you were going to drool on her T-shirt."

"She tried to fuck me in a bathroom." She gave a devious grin. "I do have standards, you know?"

"So the smoking after sex was a lie?" Carmen hoped her relief wasn't so obvious.

"No, I said I always smoke after sex *among* a few other reasons that I would keep to myself." Gin trailed a finger along the edge of Carmen's jeans. "She said her pet peeve was smokers. So I smoked one just for her. I don't take kindly to women who think I'm that easy."

Carmen kissed her again. "Tell me, Gin. Would you like to be *easy* with me tonight?"

Gin smiled up at her. "That depends. Will that *easiness* be before midnight?"

"You wouldn't have it any other way, would you?" Carmen reached for her hand.

Chapter Seventeen

Gin expected to be shoved into Carmen's car, driven home, then rode. Instead, Carmen took her hand and led them down the sidewalk.

Neither spoke as they slowly passed the lit storefronts, then went farther, past the town clock, across the street where the path wove around a fountain that had been tinted orange for early fall. Then farther still, along the line of oak trees wrapped in white lights.

Finally, Carmen broke the silence. "Teresa, huh?"

Gin rolled her eyes. "Yep. I told you my judge of character was broken."

"Did you know she was suspended two years ago for almost the same thing?"

"No." Gin wanted to correct her, to tell her that wasn't true because they had still been together. But that was the year her life had been warped out of frame, the year Teresa had fucked their relationship to a close. There was no telling what she'd done after Gin walked the hell away. "What for?"

"I don't know all the details, but rumor said a high rank stopped for breakfast with a few other important people and intercepted the cashier taking a coffee order out to Teresa's patrol car." Carmen chuckled. "Guess he didn't take too kindly to her fucking on his dime in a government-issued patrol car."

Gin gasped. The bank teller. The day she'd caught Teresa in action. The day she'd turned her back and walked away. The day she'd sworn off women in uniform, like the very one she was holding hands with right now.

What ever was she thinking?

Sex. Sex was all she was thinking about. No love. No commitment. No jealousy. No problem.

"Karma." It was the only word Gin could find. The bitch had gotten what she deserved almost immediately. It made her happy. But above the thrill of knowing Teresa had gotten busted, that if she'd stayed around a few more minutes she would have watched karma in action, she wanted to get this night started with Carmen on her knees. A few times. "You know, you don't have to court me. I'm pretty *easy* once I've said yes," she said with a quick squeeze of Carmen's hand, which felt comfortable in her grasp.

"You have something against walking?"

"No. Not really. But that *yes* equates to a much better workout, wouldn't you agree?"

"Tell me, Gin. Why do you really go on all these dates? We both know it's not for a paycheck. You have the golden ticket parked in your garage."

Gin shrugged. "Boredom?" She couldn't admit that after all the shit with Teresa, after witnessing a commitment being torn to shreds, she was still hellbound to find someone to spend the rest of her life with.

"Bored people adopt puppies, take up knitting, join a local garden club. They don't serial date."

"Coming from someone who serial fucks, I'll pass on the judgment. Besides, my way doesn't break hearts." Gin could hear the bite in her words.

Carmen stopped and stared down into those mysterious eyes. "I've never broken a single heart in my life."

"That you know of," Gin said.

Carmen considered her words. Her own ego was a bit beaten right now. Had she done the same to someone else unknowingly? Not knowing ate at her. She'd gone to such great measures to ensure that result never happened, and it saddened her to think she might have missed a sign or let one slip through her hands.

She started walking again. "So you think some staged dramatic ending to a bad date, never calling again, never saying why there wouldn't be a second date, and possibly reading about your failures in a public newspaper, even if the names are changed, compares to having a night of sex where both participants know it's nothing more than what it is? Just sex."

"Sex is personal. It's affectionate. Call it a fuck. Call it whatever you want, but it's still personal." Gin glanced up at Carmen. "Not many women think like you and I. They can't have sex once, or more, and walk away without a mental bruise."

Gin's words stung more than they should. Did she think Carmen was emotionless? "So you and I are different from the rest of the pack? Heartless? Is that what you're saying?"

Gin shook her head. "No. Only one of us has a fuck habit. I don't cross the line."

"You crossed the line with me."

Good Lord, how she'd crossed that line. And wanted to cross it again. If only she could persuade Carmen that she could take her late night walk another time.

"True. I did. But you're hard. Tough. I'm pretty sure you'll move on with life without a single thought of me. You're Carmen, after all. The hero with her own stool." Gin grinned up at Carmen although the thought of her waiting for the next piece of ass while sitting on that stool rubbed her wrong.

Carmen stopped again and stepped into her. "But will you? Think of me? Wasn't that your point? That fucking is personal and someone always gets hurt?"

Gin gently put her arms around Carmen's neck. "I think I'll manage just fine. Don't you worry your heroic little head about me. Now, can we get back to the *yes*?"

Even as Carmen was capturing those lips, she knew Gin was wrong about one thing. She was never going to forget Gin. Never going to forget their time together. Never going to forget how alive their time made her feel.

Gin moaned against her mouth, and her fingers wove into Carmen's hair, pulling her closer, her tongue dancing with Carmen's.

Finally, she pulled away and took Gin's hand again. They fit well together. She wished it wasn't so, but the fact remained. She was comfortable. Content. She hated admitting it, even to herself.

She should release Gin. She should go back to the bar, have that third beer. She should buy one for the sexy little blonde. Then she should take her home like she would have any other night of her life. Like she had planned for this very night.

Instead, she kept walking, because deep down, she knew that's exactly what she wanted to do. This was exactly where she wanted to be.

"My turn for the questions," Gin announced.

"Go for it."

"Why do you serial fuck? I mean, let's face it. You're a hottie. Not too bad in bed. A true hero. You'd be a great catch. Don't you want to join your buddies in the settled down department?"

"That life isn't on my radar. Call it a family curse, handed down for generations." She looked down at Gin with a teasing grin. "I'm not to be blamed for my DNA."

"Smartass." Gin bumped her with her shoulder. "You're saying you have been cursed to never find love?"

"I wish it was that simple. I guess you could say, I'm cursed to be a hero inside and out. That means fighting to protect a heart with as much vigor as I fight an inferno."

"You're afraid of breaking someone's heart? Coming from a woman who has her own stool?"

Carmen looked down over her. "That stool bothers you, doesn't it?"

"It feels hypocritical, that's all."

Yes. That stool bothered her. She had fucked the woman who owned that stool. A woman she would have normally snubbed her nose up at and kept walking. Instead, like the idiot she was, she'd invited her into her bed.

And she wanted to do it again right now. If only Carmen would U-turn them back to the parking lot.

Carmen shrugged. "You know the truth about that stool now. No lies. No secrets. Equals no broken hearts." She drew in a deep breath and let it out slowly. "The odds of my career taking me out of the equation are tremendous. Those odds were against my last four generations. Their pictures adorn the firehouse walls. I am cursed to be the next photo in the frame. Why would I want to take a heart down with me?"

Gin didn't respond. She couldn't. The core of Carmen had just been laid on a silver platter for her. The revelation was like a punch in the gut. Carmen wasn't just a hero to her firehouse, to her community. She was a true hero. The silent kind. The ones who worked quietly behind the scenes. She'd made a moral obligation to save broken hearts.

To save them from herself.

An hour later, Carmen sat on the foot of the bed and pulled Gin to stand between her legs.

She lifted Gin's shirt and feathered kisses across her stomach.

Gin instinctively wove her fingers into that tousled hair, thinking about their conversation. She wasn't sure how she felt about getting to know a piece of Carmen. A secret piece of her.

Sex had been simple with her before today. Before she knew what kind of heart she possessed. Sex had been just that. Sex.

With Carmen's mouth tasting, exploring, it felt different. Not like sex. Like…making love.

She didn't like it. But she couldn't move as Carmen unsnapped her jeans and pushed the zipper down. The kisses followed the opening.

What had happened to their rushed time together? What had happened to that drive for the orgasm? Why had she been so quiet during their walk back to Delaney's? What had she been thinking? Was she regretting that she'd shared that little piece of herself with Gin?

Carmen pushed Gin's jeans down over her hips and pressed her mouth against her panties, her breath hot.

Gin tightened the grip in the strands of her hair. Carmen's teeth pulled at her underwear. She wanted her to hurry. Wanted her to continue to take this slow, leisure exploration. It felt good. Felt so right. Fuck. She didn't know what she wanted.

Carmen glanced up at her, those sexy brown eyes hungry and devouring. Did she know how sexy she was? Did she know that she would likely make a great life partner for someone? It sucked that she truly believed that some family curse had blocked her path.

She pushed Gin's panties down over her hips as well and slicked a finger into the vee of her thighs.

Gin held her breath as that single digit flicked at her clit for several seconds, then she pushed farther, adding another finger, teasing her opening, spreading her, teasing again.

She closed her eyes as Carmen pushed inside, filling her, driving deeper, pulling out to the tips, and driving in again, filling her, driving in, pulling out to the tips, driving in again.

With a hiss, she fisted her fingers even tighter as the orgasm scrambled to the surface. There was a new meaning to the word easy. Carmen was making her pleasure and release entirely too easy.

Carmen kept fucking her, driving, driving, driving, until Gin lifted onto the tip of her toes, her orgasm teetering dangerously, gloriously, on the edge.

Suddenly, Carmen stood. She drove her fingers in, held for several seconds while Gin clenched around her, then pulled out, her thumb teasing her clit. Then again. And again. Drilling and driving and vibrating, watching Gin with a curious expression.

"Let it go, sexy."

Gin's orgasm ripped through her body at the sound of Carmen's command, at those pleading eyes.

She captured Gin's lips and swallowed her cries of release.

Carmen woke to the sensual weight of Gin's legs draped across her hip. Her forehead was pressed into Carmen's neck. Her breath was featherlight across Carmen's chest.

Right. This felt so right. So comfortable. So relaxed and amazing.

Gin hadn't kicked her out last night. She couldn't. She'd been in a sex induced coma long before Carmen had settled into the coziness of their tangled web of arms and legs. This time, she hadn't wanted to leave. If it cost her another punch to her ego, then so be it.

As right as this felt, as precious as it appeared, she knew this moment was ticking to a close. Gin deserved so much more. One day, she'd find just the person who wouldn't need to leave. Who wouldn't be afraid of breaking her heart with a family curse. She was working so hard to find that person.

But today, Carmen wanted to feel normal. Wanted to be normal. If only for pretend. If only for a day. The wheels were already in motion. A simple text sent long after Gin had passed out, ensured her posse would be on the scene to put Gin's trouble in the trash in another hour or two. If there was anyone who could rip a car apart and put it back together, it was her fellow firefighters.

Everyone off duty for the day would be in this yard, pulling together as a family should, and together, they were going to bring that beautiful ride back to life or else it couldn't be done.

She didn't know the whole story behind the car, or the full reason it had to be used to save the business, only that it was important to Gin. And for some reason, that was important to Carmen.

Gin stirred but didn't open her eyes. Her breathing changed. "I refuse to adult today."

Carmen couldn't resist nuzzling her cheek against Gin's head. She hated this felt so nice. Hated that her heart felt it, too. This was the exact reason she didn't stay. Ever. Why she kept her relationships brief and to the point. Because she might fall. The very thing she was doing right now. Falling.

"Good, because you inadvertently agreed to let a friend of mine come look at the car, and to a cookout. Here."

"No, I didn't." Gin lifted her head to look at Carmen.

Gin's hair was twisted into messy thick curls around her face. She resembled a person who had been fucked all night. Because she had been.

She was beautiful. Even with her expression masked in defiance, she was breathtaking. What a shame that someone had broken her heart. What a shame she would forever look for the bad in everyone. That she would trust no one for a while longer.

She pushed the hair away from Gin's face and kissed her. All the way to her toes, she felt the connection. It was so raw. So unexpected.

Gin moaned against her mouth as if she'd felt the same electric energy, and arched hard against Carmen's leg.

The kiss deepened into sexual hunger. Gin ground against her.

Carmen wasn't sure today was going to be enough. If even another night would satisfy the uncontrollable hunger that seemed never ending where Gin was concerned.

She felt so good arching into Carmen. So responsive.

Carmen shoved Gin onto her back, kneed her legs apart, pushed a hand between their bodies, searching for her wet and warm center, then drove inside.

Gin hissed and threw her head back. "You're a damn machine. Don't you have an off switch?"

Carmen bucked into her again, driving deep. She wondered the same thing. Gin was drawing out pieces of her she didn't know existed. Fact was, she didn't want to stop. She wanted Gin just like this, naked, wet, panting, again, and again. All day. All night.

"You started it. Now, say yes." Carmen pulled out to her fingertips and pushed back inside.

"To what?" Gin wrapped her arms around Carmen's neck and pulled her close, her hips lunging up to meet every stroke.

"Cookout."

"Yes." Gin bucked and bit into Carmen's shoulder. "Yes. Fuck. Yes."

Carmen bucked faster, driving Gin against the mattress until she screamed out and quivered in Carmen's arms.

An hour later, after a shower that included Carmen on her knees, with Gin begging for an end once again, they leaned against the kitchen counter. Someone knocked on the door.

"Is that your friend?" Gin asked as she bit off another bite of toast, completely in awe of her sexual thirst.

She'd barely slept at all with so much sex taking place. Glorious sex. Orgasms that were just as robust the last time as they had been the first. She shouldn't be able to walk, let alone get turned on by the sight of Carmen walking around in a sports bra. If she had to look at all that sexiness the entire day, her friend was going to get more than a view of an engine.

An engine Gin was still uptight about. Did she want a stranger picking and poking at such a precious commodity? Could they do any more harm than was already done?

Carmen leaned over the island counter and pressed a kiss against Gin's lips. "Give or take a few." She shoved away and disappeared into the foyer.

Gin listened to the front door open and then voices filled the room.

"What's up, Maverick? You shouldn't have gotten all dressed up for us." Gin recognized Daniel's voice.

"Got tools. Will travel," another voice said.

"Nate's on his way with the hoist," another voice announced, spiking Gin's worry.

More voices mingled around each other as Daniel breezed into the kitchen and dropped several bags of takeout on the counter. "Gin! Hey, doll."

He came around the counter and pushed a kiss against her cheek. "Thanks for hosting the cookout. Beth is gathering the female troops as we speak. Hope you like gossip and snot-nosed punks."

Gin opened her mouth to protest while more men filed into the room, politely saying hello, plucking biscuits from the bag, sitting on stools, the counter, some casually perched against the wall, chatting with each other like they hung out in her kitchen every day. Soon, there was barely standing room.

Was she supposed to love this as much as she did? Was she supposed to feel an emotional pull while these men, Carmen's family, treated her like she'd been among them her whole life.

She was an only child and had longed for siblings. Instantly, she felt like their little sister. It made her heart swell with pride.

Hours later, the driveway was full of shirtless firemen barking orders at each other. But one in particular stood out against all the rest. Carmen in an oily T-shirt, her hair amuck, her tanned face streaked in black.

Gin had never seen anything more sexy, and she knew beyond a shadow of a doubt that today, tonight, would be the last of her time she could share with Carmen.

She'd made her intentions clear. There were no romantic openings in her future. There never would be. She had her foot planted on the floor on the subject for reasons legitimate and honorable. Even though she would pass through this life single, never knowing what having a committed relationship felt like, it was her life and Gin would never try to sway her from that path.

What she would do is exit the situation and wish her a happy future.

For herself, she was going to finish those dates, get those articles complete, and then she was going to find a way to let her guard down, to trust again.

She wanted to go on a date. A real one.

She deserved that. The exact thing happening in her own front yard. Friends and family helping each other. A lover would be among them. A spouse. A wife. Maybe even a kid although that wasn't a deal breaker in either direction.

But this, all of it, the feeling of being complete and happy, she wanted as a permanent structure in her life. She damn well would have it.

Time seemed to fly while firemen wives showed up with bags of groceries. They all treated her like this was a weekend ritual. Her house was filled with laughter, children playing. It was the most beautiful sound in the world.

Or so she thought.

The sputter of an engine broke everyone into silence.

Gin started for the garage door. The sound sputtered again.

She made it to the door just in time to hear the engine purr to life.

The men cheered, high fiving each other, while Gin stood astounded by such a sweet sound.

The tears came next. She hadn't expected them, but damn if they didn't spring to her eyes on their own.

Not for happiness. She was anything but happy about that sound.

The sound, the gentleness, the beauty of it, made her sad.

Soon, she would never hear that sound again. Carmen, as thoughtful as she had been, had just sealed her decision. Whether Gin was ready or not.

When the night had finally come to a close, when the yard was free of firemen and their beautiful families, when the house was no longer filled with women chatting about school pickup lines and soccer drama, when children were no longer running in and out begging for another squeeze juice, Gin missed the sound so bad she yearned for its return. Craved it.

She wanted that every day in her life. She wanted a best friend who never knocked. She wanted the neighbors borrowing sugar and milk and eggs. She wanted a grill in her backyard that her spouse was the master of.

She wanted to miss someone. She wanted to think about them all day with tight eagerness to get home to them every night. She wanted an inappropriate text to make her wet.

She wanted a fucking rose.

And those things, that life, that commitment, could never be present with a woman like Carmen.

So tonight, she just wanted the last piece of Carmen.

The raw sex that connected them.

Tomorrow, she would think about her future. The car. The station. Her life.

Tomorrow.

Without saying a word, Carmen took her hand and led her toward the bedroom.

She could read the same conclusion in her eyes.

It was comforting to know that Carmen knew it, too.

CHAPTER EIGHTEEN

"Hey, Maverick," Phil yelled from his perch on the couch. "How's the studying coming along?"

Carmen looked up from the corner table where she'd been hiding most of the day, her fire inspector book open in front of her.

The last few months had been hard. Hard to admit that she wanted more out of life than one-night stands. Hard to admit that she no longer wanted to follow in her family's cursed footsteps. Hard to admit that she wanted someone who didn't want her in return. Hard to admit she was lost. Had been from the second she walked away from Gin's house knowing they would never share another night together.

It had taken every ounce of willpower she possessed not to turn around and go back into that house, to return to those warm tousled bedsheets, and drag Gin into her arms.

By far, the hardest thing she'd ever done was put the car in reverse and back out of the driveway. Hard was her middle name. She excelled at hard. Yet, someone soft, with a hardened heart, had broken her down.

She no longer wanted to be alone in this beautiful world.

Gin had made her see that. Had forced Carmen to open her eyes to life outside her sheltered, comfortable, never going to let another heart go down with her, box. And once she was on the outside looking in, she knew she no longer wanted to be a fireman. No longer wanted to be that picture in a frame.

The day she'd gone back to the bookstore, searched for a reasonable explanation, and found the proof she was looking for, had assured her the thrill she'd been looking for all along was reachable. She could step outside the footsteps of her family, with her head held high, and take a different path. A path that could include the heart of another. A path that wouldn't break the heart of anyone.

Being a fire inspector was an honorable position. An honorable way to live life. She was still a hero. Unafraid to be a hero. She didn't need a fire to prove that. But recently she'd become more afraid of dying all alone, of never knowing what it was like to commit herself to another.

She wanted to do that with Gin. Gin was the one she craved. She was the one Carmen couldn't stop thinking about. The one she never wanted to stop thinking about. She wanted Gin more than she'd wanted anything else in her life.

Carmen had been the reason the inspectors had changed their conclusion, the reason the investigation had uncovered footage of the arsonist in several locations before and after his little criminal activities, and he was now behind bars where he deserved to be.

For the first time, she was in love. In love with a hero-hater who made her want to change. To be something more than a hero. To be her hero.

She wanted to change her life, the fears and insecurities that came with that life. The fears that kept her distanced from commitment.

"It's coming along," Carmen answered.

"What time is your test tomorrow?" Phil turned around to look at her.

"Eight."

"You'll do great. No sweat." He winked. "You'll be working from a boring office in no time. Which reminds me, Steph has already set the wheels in motion for this weekend. You ready, Ms. Never Going to Fall in Love?"

The mention of being in love made her heart skip. It was a great feeling. Amazing, actually. But the mention of the weekend made her gut tighten into a strangled knot. The moment she was going to propose a commitment to Gin. Disguised as Gin's last date.

Carmen had been shocked to learn that Gin hadn't completed her contract. Instead, Steph said she'd been focused on selling the car, as well as the business. The choice had been too great, too deep, so Steph said the choice for Gin had been obvious all along. She sold them both.

And with Steph and Phil carrying Cupid's arrow this weekend, with Patrick working the website to score Carmen that last date, she only had herself to fear. Fear that was eating her alive. What if Gin rejected her? What if Gin truly had her talons hooked in the belief that every hero was a cheater and always would be a cheater? That every hero was a cheater even if they weren't.

Her life was about to change in the most drastic way. Instead of rushing into a fire, she would be investigating the cause. Instead of dashing for her gear and diving into a fire truck with the sound of the sirens, she would be taking notes on the charred remains. Instead of dragging a lifeless body from a fire, she would be wielding a pen and making inspection rounds.

Would she feel less of a hero? Would she regret the change?

The way she felt right now, anxious to get this test in her rearview mirror so her future could become her present, she didn't see how she could regret anything. She was excited. Ready. In love.

That, above all else, was the most incredible part. Carmen was in love. The thought seemed so surreal. Even more surreal was the fact that someone, a person who couldn't stand her, who looked at her as anything but a hero, had busted down her need to be alone forever.

And Gin had no clue she'd done it.

"I'm ready," Carmen said.

And she was. Ready. Ready to show up at Gin's date, her last date, *as* her date. She couldn't wait to see her face again. Couldn't wait to take her out on a date. A real date. She wanted to walk through a park hand in hand again. Wanted ice cream on a boring Sunday when the rest of the world was watching football. She wanted to surprise her with a puppy at Christmas. Wanted to watch her blow out candles on her birthday. Wanted to buy her a bouquet of flowers for absolutely no reason at all.

She was ready to commit herself to Gin for the rest of her life.

God, she'd never been so ready.

❖

Steph fell onto the couch beside Gin and propped her feet up on the coffee table. They'd spent the whole day, almost the whole week, moving the last of her personal inventory from the station back to her house.

"So, tell me. What's it like being rich?" Steph wiggled her eyebrows.

Holy shit. She was rich. Not millionaire rich, but after barely having spending money for years, she sure felt like a millionaire.

After watching the Porsche leave the property on a rollback, after closing on the station at the lawyer's office, and moving boxes nonstop, shedding tear after tear, she hadn't stopped long enough to soak in the fact that she wouldn't have to worry about bills for a very long time. Who was she kidding? She wouldn't have to worry about bills for the rest of her life if she was smart with the money.

The burden of the fight was over. No more worries. No more wondering how she was going to pay for an order. No more pondering how she was going to pay the utility bills. No more worries at all.

Well, except for the part that she would be rich and alone. That part she'd have to work on. Eventually.

Right now, she was mentally depleted. Everything was finally catching up to her. The car, gone. The station, gone. Selling the station had been the hardest. The car had gone to loving hands, to a person who would treasure her.

She knew she wouldn't have the same luxury with the station.

A rich businessman had promised he was going to incorporate the structure into his new project, make it a gatekeeper's lodge for the automotive plant that would soon start construction. That was a lie, she knew, but it gave her peace anyway.

Her grandmother's adoration for a car was no more important than her grandfather's love for the station. They were equally important, and because of that, she'd chosen not to choose either. She'd sold them both.

Financially, she was sitting pretty for a long time. Time enough to breathe in some relaxation. Take a vacation. Hell, she could go all out and buy a little piece of property on the coast if she wanted. There were no chains to bind her now. Not a single thing to hold her back.

Steph was going to do the U-Haul thing very soon. That move was inevitable. She and Phil were practically inseparable. Patrick wasn't far behind her. His new love interest finally had a name. Seth, a cutie who was a full-time choreographer and part-time drag show coordinator, who adored Patrick. He'd snagged himself a good one, and Gin was thrilled for him.

Soon, without any fault of their own, they were going to move in separate directions from her. The single one. She would be invited to Sunday dinners, maybe a special night at the club. But sooner or later, the time they spent together would be less and less.

It was part of life. That's the way the ball bounced when you were a third wheel. As bummed as she was, she was happy for them.

One day, hopefully sooner rather than later, she was going to have the exact same thing. She was going to have a better half. An equal. Until then, she was going to live this thing called life.

And when she bumped into Carmen at one of those cookouts, at one of those special events, she was going to hug her like a long lost friend, as if they hadn't spent some incredible time between the sheets, as if Carmen's name had never slipped past her lips in ecstasy. As if she hadn't secretly fallen in love with her somewhere along their short time together.

Yes. She'd done that. She'd fallen in love. Fallen in love with yet another hero. Seemed Carmen wasn't the only one with a curse. She was obviously cursed to fall in love with all the wrong people for the rest of her life.

Unlike Carmen, Gin wasn't going to run anymore. She was going to pick up the pieces, she was going to take a deep breath, and then she was going to try her luck at love again. This time, she wasn't going to dig for the skeletons. She wasn't going to mistrust immediately. She wasn't going to look for all the wrong things. She wasn't going to run from the heroes. She was going to face them head-on. Maybe if she got lucky enough she'd recognize the true hero before she drew her sword. Before she went for blood.

If Carmen could go through life alone, protecting hearts even from herself, Gin could have hope that she too would find that love again. She would trust wide open. She would love with a wild abandon. Once again, she would give it everything she had.

"I'm not sure." Gin pulled a pillow to her chest and crossed her legs. "It hasn't sunk in yet."

"I think you should take us all on a cruise to celebrate your success. Caribbean, Bahamas, anything tropical, is my preference, so you know." Steph wiggled her brow.

"I don't feel very successful. Feels like I just pawned off my life."

Steph patted her leg. "Give it time, baby. Let the relaxation settle in. You'll see being stress free was well worth it."

The computer pinged a familiar tune from across the room. Match-Us. Someone had sent her an invitation.

"Hey, that's a date request!" Steph squealed and rolled off the couch. She darted for the laptop and brought it back to Gin. "You still have one last date to do. Open it!"

Gin had forgotten to cancel her subscription during all of the chaos. She had no desire to go on any date, even if was the last one. She had no reason to go at all.

"No." Gin closed the lid.

Steph tugged the laptop from her grasp. "You have to. You owe Cynthia one more article."

"You just reminded me that I was rich." Gin scoffed. "Why would I waste my time? It was all useless anyway."

"Because that's the kind of awesome person you are." Steph leaned down and rubbed her head in Gin's lap. "And because you know my man gets totally turned on when I'm in action mode. Do it for me, bestest friend. Do it for my sex life."

Gin pushed her head away. "You're a freak."

"Me a freak? I'm not the one who slept with my archenemy. More than once." Steph blew an air kiss at her.

The mention of Carmen settled heat against her cheeks. God, how she'd slept with Carmen. The feel of her hadn't disappeared yet. The memories were forever going to scald her.

"How's she doing?" Gin shouldn't ask, but she needed to know. Steph had been tight-lipped about her, and Gin couldn't bring herself to ask. Until now.

"Didn't I tell you? She's changing careers. She's going to be a fire inspector," Steph said, matter-of-fact, as if no big deal.

That was a huge deal. Carmen loved being a firefighter. And fuck if she wasn't damn good at it.

"Really?" No, Steph hadn't told her a damn thing. Especially not that.

"Really." Steph gave a tight nod. "The sexy fireman took herself off the hero market and hung up her helmet."

"Why?"

"No clue." Steph shrugged. "Something about breaking her own curse. Whatever that means."

Gin mentally smiled as she recalled their conversation. How she was cursed to protect hearts forever. How she could never take a heart down with her when the curse came to claim her.

If only she could have protected Gin's heart. If only Gin had protected her own. She wouldn't be thinking about Carmen right now, every day, every night, all the freaking time. Wouldn't be pondering the what-ifs. What if they hadn't been on separate paths in life? What if Gin hadn't been so determined to hate heroes? What if Carmen hadn't been so determined that a curse truly did exist? What if? There were so many of them.

But if Carmen had suddenly decided to change her career, did that mean that she had met someone who was worth breaking the family chains? Was there any other reason she would step out of a career that was handed down through generations of being a fireman? Something she was so fucking hot doing?

Gin's stomach tightened into a hard knot. Of course she'd met someone. There was no other reasonable explanation. Great. Just great.

That meant the next time she saw Carmen, there would be a beauty hanging off her arm. Gin wouldn't be able to look at Carmen the same. She would hate the woman, no matter if she was the sweetest person alive.

She would hate her because she had exactly what Gin wanted.

Because she had Carmen. The one she wanted. Yes. She'd wanted Carmen. Fuck. How had she let this happen to herself? She'd fought so hard, for so long, to avoid this very outcome.

Steph flipped the top back open on the laptop. "Date. Come on. Do the last one for me. Do it for my sex life. Pwease." Her bottom lip rolled out.

Gin huffed, took the laptop, and clicked the message icon. "You're impossible."

She opened the invitation. The woman didn't even have a profile picture. She wanted to meet tonight at seven at a little Mexican restaurant downtown. Casual attire.

"Ooh. She's a mystery. I like it," Steph said. "I'm free tonight. So is Phil. Do it! In and out, thirty minutes, tops."

Gin normally didn't waste her time on someone who didn't waste their time adding a photo. But right now, she just wanted everything in her life concluded. She wanted to be free from all obligations.

The car. Done.

The station. Done.

The contract. It was the only thing left. That last date.

She thought of Carmen. Making a change. Moving on with life. No doubt with someone who made her need to make a change, because without that change, the hero couldn't be a hero.

Her stomach flipped again. How could she miss someone she truly never had? How could she want someone who wasn't available?

Damn. She needed to move on. Maybe the woman behind this blank profile would be the one she'd been looking for. Maybe she would make Gin's heart sputter out of control. Maybe, just maybe, she'd be the one Gin had been waiting for for so damn long.

Yes. It was time to move on. Time to lift her head out of self-pity and stop acting like the world owed her something as if it had anything to do with her broken heart.

She hit the respond button.

Accepted.

"Yay!" Steph squealed and grabbed her cell phone off the coffee table. "Let me text Phil and tell him the good news."

Gin didn't feel like it was good news.

As a matter of fact, she felt rather nauseous. Not because she was going on a date. Not because it was the last one. Not because she had no clue what her date even looked like.

Because Carmen wasn't, nor would she ever be, her before or after midnight fuck again.

Chapter Nineteen

Gin stepped into the Mexican restaurant and breathed in the spicy aroma of fajitas. She didn't want to be here. Didn't want to be on a date at all, even if it was the last one. Match-Us was a complete joke. The articles were a joke. So was this date tonight.

Mentally, she wasn't here. Mentally, her thoughts were on Carmen. She wanted to talk to her. She wanted to hear her story. Wanted to know if she was excited to make a career change. Wanted to know why, after generations of firemen, she'd wanted to change. Wanted to hear that she hadn't found someone. That she wasn't doing the same things to them that she'd done to Gin.

Then she wanted to crawl inside her T-shirt. Yes. That's what she wanted to do. She wanted to crawl inside Carmen's firehouse T-shirt. She wanted to drag it off with her teeth. Then she wanted Carmen to fuck her own name out of Gin's mouth.

Again.

Her insides throbbed from the image.

A young hostess wearing a bright smile and all black attire, greeted Gin, dragging the heated thoughts from her mind.

"Hi, sweetie." The girl pasted Gin in pale chocolate eyes. "How many will be joining you tonight?"

Carmen had brown eyes. They were sexy brown eyes.

She inhaled, insulted by her self-control. Just one. Just one useless, waste of time date. "I'm meeting someone. Vic?"

"Yes, ma'am. She has a booth reserved in the adjacent room." She pulled two menus from a slot under the desk. "Please follow me."

Gin trailed behind her until the woman stopped at a booth and motioned for her to sit. She scooted onto the seat. "Thank you."

The hostess walked away while Gin inspected the rest of the room. Four tables had been joined together in a single row down the center. Three reserved signs were perched in the middle. Hopefully, the party that needed that many chairs wouldn't be here while she got this last date out of the way.

A bar lined with diamond shaped cubicles adorned the entire length of the back wall, all filled with liquor bottles. Happy hour was over, and Gin wasn't surprised to see that only one person was drinking.

She almost chuckled. Last date. This was her last date. What the hell was she thinking? She didn't need the money anymore. Didn't need one last date to prove that this town didn't have what she was looking for.

Well, minus one fireman. A fireman who had burned her with a simple touch. A fireman who was afraid to love, to commit, to be loved, who might have found someone to change her mind about wanting to love and commit and to be loved, after all. A fireman she couldn't shake from her mind no matter how hard she tried.

Maybe it was time to blow this place. This city. Maybe find a quaint little one red light town where everyone knew each other, where children graduated from the same high school that their grandparents had attended. Basically, the same life she had now. The kind of life she thought she wanted. Maybe it wasn't. Maybe that shouldn't be what she wanted.

She was living proof this atmosphere wasn't working out.

Maybe she should take a different step. She could move to a bustling city, live in a high-rise apartment with a panoramic view, where neighbors barely took notice of each other. Her weekdays would be spent working nine to five and her weekends would be spent in nightclubs where everyone was packed in like sardines.

Yeah, like she'd get to know anyone that way.

Gin's phone chirped, and she looked down to find a text from Steph.

We're here. Heading inside.

She smiled, thankful. She wouldn't have to do this last disastrous chore alone.

Not to mention, it was downright adorable how much she and Phil loved each other. Instant. It had been instant. As sad as Gin was that she was going to be lonely, she was thrilled for both of them. This is what life was all about. What it was supposed to be about. Finding love. Making memories.

One day, probably not today, maybe not tomorrow, she was going to find what she was looking for.

Today, she just wanted to get this date over with then curl up with her laptop for a final article she'd already concluded she would make as boring as humanly possible. No more wrist smacking emails from Patricia. If she wanted boring, Gin would damn well give it to her.

Steph and Phil breezed into the room, directly to the back wall without a single glance in her direction, and found two stools with a direct shot to her table.

Man, how she loved her. As well as Phil who was perfect for Steph. It sucked how much she missed them. She'd been scarce for so many weeks, hiding in her own misery. Sure, she had the excuse of kissing a beloved Porsche good-bye and lawyer meetings, but truth be told, she was terrified of bumping into Carmen. But also almost desperate at times to bump into her.

She glanced down at her watch. Fifteen minutes early. Why did she find it necessary to be so punctual? Why couldn't she be ten, twenty minutes, late like most of her dates were? She could make a dramatic entrance, where all eyes were on her.

"Gin?"

Gin turned to find Daniel's wife, Beth, staring at her. Her sweet smile made Gin homesick for a home she'd never had. Homesick for a family that wasn't hers. For Carmen's family. Homesick for a future she desperately wanted, one she might never get.

Gin stood and gave her a big hug. A hug that made her heart ache for what she didn't have. For what she wanted so bad. She wanted that loving family. Where everyone was more like brothers and sisters instead of friends and neighbors.

A family. She fucking wanted a family exactly like Carmen had. People who cared about each other. Who loved each other.

She didn't just want a family identical to Carmen's. She wanted those people. Carmen's people. The people she had liked, loved, instantly. Worse, she wanted Carmen. Damn, it felt good to admit that if only to herself. Carmen. Carmen was the one she wanted. Carmen was the one she loved. Who made her ache. Who made her angry. Who made her wet.

Carmen. The one who brought out every emotion she never knew she possessed, sometimes in a single night.

Love. She loved Carmen.

"It's so good to see you." Beth stepped out of the hug. "How have you been?"

"I've been good." Gin glanced around in hopes of seeing other familiar faces but also terrified she would see one in particular. That face would make her heart leap. And then make her wet. "Where's the rest of your crew?"

Beth pointed to the long tables. "They'll be here soon. Just getting everyone together for a little family night. You should join us. Everyone will be thrilled to see you."

Gin would have loved that so much. Instead, she was going to endure more wasted time on another date. The last date.

Then what? What did life have in store for her?

Anything. Anything she wanted it to be. That's what.

She could travel. She could spend a month in the tropics. Maybe a year. She could hook up with the locals, have sex with people she would never see again.

She could. But she was positive that every time she closed her eyes while fingers, or a mouth, coaxed her to climax, Carmen would be the virtual reality staring down over her.

"That's sweet, and I would love to, but I kind of have a date in a few minutes."

"Ooh la la," Beth said. Then she leaned in. "You know, all the guys had a wager going at the firehouse about you and Carmen becoming an item."

"Oh really?" Gin gave a nervous giggle. "Hope Daniel didn't lose your grocery money."

She and Carmen were the most unlikely people to ever become an item. But for sure, she'd envisioned it. How they would spend their weekends. How many cookouts they would host. Thanksgiving. Christmas. There would never be a dull moment in her life. She wanted that. She didn't want there to ever be a dull moment in her life.

She wanted people to joke around. People to make her laugh. She wanted to call their children her nieces and nephews. She wanted to hang out, go camping, do normal couple stuff.

"We'll see." She gave Gin a wink and moved toward the line of tables.

Gin wanted to go after her, to tell her that she and Carmen could never be anything other than passing acquaintances, that there wasn't a fat fucking chance in hell that she could ever be with another player, then she settled back against the booth. She'd already done that. Been with another player, who turned out not to be such a player. Now, here she sat, on another date, wasting her time, with that player controlling her thoughts.

She sighed. If only she'd never met Carmen. If not for Carmen, she wouldn't be missing people she would have never met. She wouldn't be mourning for a family she would have never known. The family she adored, she would have never met, if not for Carmen.

With a grunt, she checked her watch. The date wasn't due to begin for another few minutes. Why did Gin have to be so punctual? What was wrong with being fashionably late? Making an entrance without any excuse for her tardiness.

People filed into the room, their voices loud.

Robert. His wife. Two kids. More firemen she recognized from the cookout, as well as men who had occupied her garage, stepped into the room.

One by one, they all approached her with hugs and kisses, greeting her like a part of the family, encouraging her to come join them. Most told her to bring the date after she confessed that was her reason for being there.

How she wished she could. How she wished her life was different. That she was a fireman's wife, a fire inspector's wife, sitting at that table, sharing their love.

She checked her watch again. A few more minutes. If her date was on time, she could blow this joint in less than ten, have a detailed article written in an hour, and be done with the likes of Patricia and Cynthia. Patricia could move on to another author who was less inclined to tell it like it was.

Laughter filled the room while the silverware on the table held Gin transfixed. How could she love and adore people she barely knew? Why had they been so welcoming to her, making her feel like she'd been a part of their crew her whole life? Why did they all have to be so amazing?

Why did Carmen have to be such a player? A player who didn't play.

Gin snickered out loud. The sound was swallowed by the chatter of the firemen and their families.

The irony of the night was funny. She was soon going to be across this table from a woman, with another woman on her mind. With that other woman's family only feet away from her, where she'd much rather be. That other woman, she couldn't rip from her mind. That other woman had stolen something from her. Something that had been locked down tight. That something had been untouchable. Yet, Carmen had touched it. Tasted it. Then stole it.

How ironic was that? The one person, the one type of person, who shouldn't have been able to get close enough to cause harm, had caused the most damage.

And she had no clue she'd done it. Would never have a clue.

Gin took a deep breath, hating the naughty thoughts that seemed to be a permanent gallery of rolling images in her mind, and checked her watch again.

Five after. Her date was late. This was grounds for leaving. Her article would be short and sweet, and as she promised herself, boring. Wouldn't Patricia love that?

The laughter grew louder. That sweet sound aggravated Gin even more. She checked her watch again. Seven after.

There was no use waiting. This whole night wasn't going to end well anyway.

Gin turned to leave the booth and found Carmen staring down at her, her body blocking the edge of the seat. Her white button-up shirt was untucked, ending at the crotch of her dark denim jeans, beckoning Gin's attention to that very spot.

She sucked in a quiet breath as her heart somersaulted.

Fuck. Carmen looked so good. Her hair was longer. Still finger combed.

Gin wanted to drive herself against that body. Wanted to snake her tongue inside that mouth.

The need was so strong, she had to will herself back in control.

"Gin," Carmen whispered.

The single word was like an erotic, unspoken demand.

Heat feathered along her skin and her insides clenched down hard.

"Hi," Gin finally breathed.

So much for acting normal the next time she ran into Carmen. This, right here, right now, unable to control even a simple function like speaking, was why she needed to get the hell away from this place.

She was out of her mind if she thought she could ever act like a sane human being around Carmen again.

Without asking permission, Carmen scooted into the booth across from her. "How have you been?"

The room went quiet. The laughter vanished. Even the children went silent. The chatter was smothered with the loud ringing in Gin's ear.

"Fine," she managed.

She'd never wanted anyone as much as she wanted Carmen. She shouldn't want her. Shouldn't need her. But fuck, she did. So bad, it knotted her stomach. So bad, it made her heart ache.

She was breaking the rules. Her very own rules.

And yet, she wanted nothing more than to climb across this table, straddle Carmen's face, and buck against her until an orgasm left her boneless.

"I'm actually waiting for a date," Gin finally added just to hear something other than the silence. The words sounded fake, even hilarious, echoing back on her own ears.

"I know." Carmen toyed with the napkin around the silverware.

Gin glanced toward Steph and Phil, who had joined the table of firemen. They both looked away immediately.

When Gin looked back at Carmen, those dark eyes were on her, waiting. "Of course you do. I'll never have another secret, will I?" She tried to sound comical, but there was nothing comical about Carmen being this close to her. The too-close proximity was so fucking dangerous.

Carmen folded her hands together and steepled two fingers under her chin. "I know because I'm Vic. Your date. Your last date."

Gin gave her a smirk and thought back to her profile. Vic, in between jobs, who hated Yorkies and football. She'd assumed Vic was short of Victoria, who was recently fired, or maybe she was a habitual job hopper. Instead, was it short for Maverick who was a fireman moving into a new field?

Was it true? Was Carmen her last date? Was this like some fairy tale ending to her mission? Was that even possible considering that the rules forbid her to fall in love with a hero?

"Why?" Gin exhaled.

"You know why." Carmen slid her hands across the table and lightly touched her fingertips against Gin's. She pushed harder until Gin lifted her hand from the surface, then she wove their fingers together.

She did. She knew. Had known from the beginning. She'd felt it. Had felt it all along.

It had been spontaneous. Instant.

"I have an important question for you," Carmen whispered.

"What?"

"Are you ready to break the rules?"

She'd never been more ready for anything in her life.

In answer, she leaned across the table, eager to touch Carmen. Carmen eagerly followed, stretching for that connection.

When the table halted their progress, Carmen shoved out of the booth and jerked Gin to her feet. Their lips crushed against each other and cheers erupted around them.

Gin fisted her free hand into Carmen's shirt, pulling her closer, desperate for the whole weight of her.

"Cover the children's eyes!" Robert said.

Carmen tugged her fingers free of their hold and draped both of Gin's arms around her neck. "These belong right here. You are beyond the rescue attempts of your posse for the rest of your life."

Gin pressed her lips against Carmen's again, happy, fulfilled, in disbelief, and so eager to take the next step.

"Do you understand what I'm saying, Gin?" Carmen pressed her forehead against Gin's.

Gin smiled against her lips. "Understood."

Carmen pressed her mouth against Gin's once again, claiming and reassuring.

Someone hooted. Another howled. Another whistled.

Finally, Carmen pulled back, staring down over Gin like a prized possession. "I passed my test and broke the curse. Soon, I'll be a fire inspector."

Gin leaned back to look up into those chocolate eyes and saw a future staring back at her. A happy future. A future she could trust. "Too bad. I liked you better as a hooker."

Carmen gave her that crooked smile then pushed her mouth against Gin's ear and whispered. "I'll show you a hooker."

The End

About the Author

Larkin Rose lives in a "blink and you've missed it" town with Rose, her wife of twenty-two years, in the beautiful state of South Carolina. Together, they shared seven very active kids, who weren't allowed to read her books until they were married. They are now all grown up, married, and multiplied, making her a super Nana to eleven grandkids, too. They are still not allowed to read her books (or rather, admit it). After a four-year hiatus, she's now back writing full time.

The fantasies continue. The clatter of keys continues. And the birth of erotic creations shall carry on.

To know more, visit Larkinrose.com.

Books Available from Bold Strokes Books

Against All Odds by Kris Bryant, Maggie Cummings, M. Ullrich. Peyton and Tory escaped death once, but will they survive when Bradley's determined to make his kill rate one hundred percent? (978-1-163555-193-8)

Autumn's Light by Aurora Rey. Casual hookups aren't supposed to include romantic dinners and meeting the family. Can Mat Pero see beyond the heartbreak that led her to keep her worlds so separate, and will Graham Connor be waiting if she does? (978-1-163555-272-0)

Breaking the Rules by Larkin Rose. When Virginia and Carmen are thrown together by an embarrassing mistake they find out their stubborn determination isn't so heroic after all. (978-1-163555-261-4)

Broad Awakening by Mickey Brent. In the sequel to *Underwater Vibes*, Hélène and Sylvie find ruts in their road to eternal bliss. (978-1-163555-270-6)

Broken Vows by MJ Williamz. Sister Mary Margaret must reconcile her divided heart or risk losing a love that just might be heaven sent. (978-1-163555-022-1)

Flesh and Gold by Ann Aptaker. Havana, 1952, where art thief and smuggler Cantor Gold dodges gangland bullets and mobsters' schemes while she searches Havana's steamy Red Light district for her kidnapped love. (978-1-163555-153-2)

Isle of Broken Years by Jane Fletcher. Spanish noblewoman Catalina de Valasco is in peril, even before the pirates holding her for ransom sail into seas destined to become known as the Bermuda Triangle. (978-1-163555-175-4)

Love Like This by Melissa Brayden. Hadley Cooper and Spencer Adair set out to take the fashion world by storm. If only they knew their hearts were about to be taken. (978-1-163555-018-4)

Secrets On the Clock by Nicole Disney. Jenna and Danielle love their jobs helping endangered children, but that might not be enough to stop them from breaking the rules by falling in love. (978-1-163555-292-8)

Unexpected Partners by Michelle Larkin. Dr. Chloe Maddox tries desperately to deny her attraction for Detective Dana Blake as they flee from a serial killer who's hunting them both. (978-1-163555-203-4)

A Fighting Chance by T. L. Hayes. Will Lou be able to come to terms with her past to give love a fighting chance? (978-1-163555-257-7)

Chosen by Brey Willows. When the choice is adapt or die, can love save us all? (978-1-163555-110-5)

Death Checks In by David S. Pederson. Despite Heath's promises to Alan to not get involved, Heath can't resist investigating a shopkeeper's murder in Chicago, which dashes their plans for a romantic weekend getaway. (978-1-163555-329-1)

Gnarled Hollow by Charlotte Greene. After they are invited to study a secluded nineteenth-century estate, a former English professor and a group of historians discover that they will have to fight against the unknown if they have any hope of staying alive. (978-1-163555-235-5)

Jacob's Grace by C.P. Rowlands. Captain Tag Becket wants to keep her head down and her past behind her, but her feelings for AJ's second-in-command, Grace Fields, makes keeping secrets next to impossible. (978-1-163555-187-7)

On the Fly by PJ Trebelhorn. Hockey player Courtney Abbott is content with her solitary life until visiting concert violinist Lana Caruso makes her second-guess everything she always thought she wanted. (978-1-163555-255-3)

Passionate Rivals by Radclyffe. Professional rivalry and long-simmering passions create a combustible combination when Emmett McCabe and Sydney Stevens are forced to work together, especially when past attractions won't stay buried. (978-1-163555-231-7)

Proxima Five by Missouri Vaun. When geologist Leah Warren crash-lands on a preindustrial planet and is claimed by its tyrant, Tiago, will clan warrior Keegan's love for Leah give her the strength to defeat him? (978-1-163555-122-8)

Racing Hearts by Dena Blake. When you cross a hot-tempered race car mechanic with a reckless cop, the result can only be spontaneous combustion. (978-1-163555-251-5)

Shadowboxer by Jessica L. Webb. Jordan McAddie is prepared to keep her street kids safe from a dangerous underground protest group, but she isn't prepared for her first love to walk back into her life. (978-1-163555-267-6)

The Tattered Lands by Barbara Ann Wright. As Vandra and Lilani strive to make peace, they slowly fall in love. With mistrust and murder surrounding them, only their faith in each other can keep their plan to save the world from falling apart. (978-1-163555-108-2)

Captive by Donna K. Ford. To escape a human trafficking ring, Greyson Cooper and Olivia Danner become players in a game of deceit and violence. Will their love stand a chance? (978-1-63555-215-7)

Crossing the Line by CF Frizzell. The Mob discovers a nemesis within its ranks, and in the ultimate retaliation, draws Stick McLaughlin from anonymity by threatening everything she holds dear. (978-1-63555-161-7)

Love's Verdict by Carsen Taite. Attorneys Landon Holt and Carly Pachett want the exact same thing: the only open partnership spot at their prestigious criminal defense firm. But will they compromise their careers for love? (978-1-63555-042-9)

Precipice of Doubt by Mardi Alexander & Laurie Eichler. Can Cole Jameson resist her attraction to her boss, veterinarian Jodi Bowman, or will she risk a workplace romance and her heart? (978-1-63555-128-0)

Savage Horizons by CJ Birch. Captain Jordan Kellow's feelings for Lt. Ali Ash have her past and future colliding, setting in motion a series of events that strands her crew in an unknown galaxy thousands of light years from home. (978-1-63555-250-8)

Secrets of the Last Castle by A. Rose Mathieu. When Elizabeth Campbell represents a young man accused of murdering an elderly woman, her investigation leads to an abandoned plantation that reveals many dark Southern secrets. (978-1-63555-240-9)

Take Your Time by VK Powell. A neurotic parrot brings police officer Grace Booker and temporary veterinarian Dr. Dani Wingate together in the tiny town of Pine Cone, but their unexpected attraction keeps the sparks flying. (978-1-63555-130-3)

The Last Seduction by Ronica Black. When you allow true love to elude you once and you desperately regret it, are you brave enough to grab it when it comes around again? (978-1-63555-211-9)

The Shape of You by Georgia Beers. Rebecca McCall doesn't play it safe, but when sexy Spencer Thompson joins her workout class, their non-stop sparring forces her to face her ultimate challenge—a chance at love. (978-1-63555-217-1)

Exposed by MJ Williamz. The closet is no place to live if you want to find true love. (978-1-62639-989-1)

Force of Fire: Toujours a Vous by Ali Vali. Immortals Kendal and Piper welcome their new child and celebrate the defeat of an old enemy, but another ancient evil is about to awaken deep in the jungles of Costa Rica. (978-1-63555-047-4)

Holding Their Place by Kelly A. Wacker. Together Dr. Helen Connery and ambulance driver Julia March, discover that goodness, love, and passion can be found in the most unlikely and even dangerous places during WWI. (978-1-63555-338-3)

Landing Zone by Erin Dutton. Can a career veteran finally discover a love stronger than even her pride? (978-1-63555-199-0)

Love at Last Call by M. Ullrich. Is balancing business, friend-ship, and love more than any willing woman can handle? (978-1-63555-197-6)

Pleasure Cruise by Yolanda Wallace. Spencer Collins and Amy Donovan have few things in common, but a Caribbean cruise offers both women an unexpected chance to face one of their greatest fears: falling in love. (978-1-63555-219-5)

Running Off Radar by MB Austin. Maji's plans to win Rose back are interrupted when work intrudes and duty calls her to help a SEAL team stop a Russian mobster from harvesting gold from the bottom of Sitka Sound. (978-1-63555-152-5)

Shadow of the Phoenix by Rebecca Harwell. In the final battle for the fate of Storm's Quarry, even Nadya's and Shay's powers may not be enough. (978-1-63555-181-5)

Take a Chance by D. Jackson Leigh. There's hardly a woman within fifty miles of Pine Cone that veterinarian Trip Beaumont can't charm, except for the irritating new cop, Jamie Grant, who keeps leaving parking tickets on her truck. (978-1-63555-118-1)

The Outcasts by Alexa Black. Spacebus driver Sue Jones is running from her past. When she crash-lands on a faraway world, the Outcast Kara might be her chance for redemption. (978-1-63555-242-3)

Alias by Cari Hunter. A car crash leaves a woman with no memory and no identity. Together with Detective Bronwen Pryce, she fights to uncover a truth that might just kill them both. (978-1-63555-221-8)

Death in Time by Robyn Nyx. Working in the past is hell on your future. (978-1-63555-053-5)

Hers to Protect by Nicole Disney. High school sweethearts Kaia and Adrienne will have to see past their differences and survive the vengeance of a brutal gang if they want to be together. (978-1-63555-229-4)

Of Echoes Born by 'Nathan Burgoine. A collection of queer fantasy short stories set in Canada from Lambda Literary Award finalist 'Nathan Burgoine. (978-1-63555-096-2)

Perfect Little Worlds by Clifford Mae Henderson. Lucy can't hold the secret any longer. Twenty-six years ago, her sister did the unthinkable. (978-1-63555-164-8)

Room Service by Fiona Riley. Interior designer Olivia likes stability, but when work brings footloose Savannah into her world and into a new city every month, Olivia must decide if what makes her comfortable is what makes her happy. (978-1-63555-120-4)

Sparks Like Ours by Melissa Brayden. Professional surfers Gia Malone and Elle Britton can't deny their chemistry on and off the beach. But only one can win… (978-1-63555-016-0)

Take My Hand by Missouri Vaun. River Hemsworth arrives in Georgia intent on escaping quickly, but when she crashes her Mercedes into the Clip 'n Curl, sexy Clay Cahill ends up rescuing more than her car. (978-1-63555-104-4)

The Last Time I Saw Her by Kathleen Knowles. Lane Hudson only has twelve days to win back Alison's heart. That is if she can gather the courage to try. (978-1-63555-067-2)

Wayworn Lovers by Gun Brooke. Will agoraphobic composer Giselle Bonnaire and Tierney Edwards, a wandering soul who can't remain in one place for long, trust in the passionate love destiny hands them? (978-1-62639-995-2)